THAT LOVE

THAT LOVE

JILLIAN DODD

Jillian Dodd Inc.
Madeira Beach, FL
Jillian Dodd is a registered trademark of Jillian Dodd Inc.

Editor: Jovana Shirley, Unforeseen Editing
Photo by: Regina Wamba
Cover Design: Mae I Design

ISBN: 978-1-946793-13-3

Books by Jillian Dodd

The Keatyn Chronicles®
USA TODAY bestselling young adult contemporary romance set in an East Coast boarding school.
Stalk Me
Kiss Me
Date Me
Love Me
Adore Me
Hate Me
Get Me
Fame
Power
Money
Sex
Love
Keatyn Unscripted
Aiden

That Boy Series
Small-town contemporary romance series about falling in love with the boy next door.
That Boy
That Wedding
That Baby
That Love
That Ring

The Love Series
Contemporary, standalone romances following the very sexy Crawford family.
Vegas Love
Broken Love

Spy Girl® Series
Young adult romance series about a young spy who just might save the world.
The Prince
The Eagle
The Society
The Valiant
The Dauntless
The Phoenix
The Echelon

PROLOGUE
14 YEARS EARLIER

Danny

"THAT KISS WAS like a freaking fairy tale," Jennifer blurts out the second our lips part.

And I have to agree with her. I've kissed a lot of girls, but I've never experienced anything quite like this. Not this crazy, instant connection.

I've definitely experienced *lust* at first sight—but *love* at first kiss?

"I'll be honest," she continues. "I was hoping to come out here for a quick roll in the sand 'cause you're hot and I'm tipsy, but, fuck, what am I supposed to do with you now, Danny Diamond?"

I smirk. Lord help me, I can think of so many things I'd like her to do to me. Except … I can't.

"As much as I'm dying to know the answer to that, I'm married," I reply, holding up my left hand in response, the wedding ring on my finger feeling like it's burning a mark into my skin. I don't know what I was thinking. I should not be on the beach with this girl. I shouldn't have even let it go this far.

But Jennifer Edwards is funny and blunt and adorable. We've been laughing our asses off since the moment we were introduced at the party.

I think about my daughter—specifically, my wife's threats to take her away from me if I ever stray.

Jennifer must see the internal struggle in my eyes. She runs her hand down my arm and says coyly, "If you can't promise forever, just promise tonight."

I suck in a deep breath, trying to slow down the hormones raging in my body. "I'm sorry. I can't. I should probably get back to the party."

"Oh, fine," she says, rolling her gorgeous eyes up toward the moon. "We'll just talk. Hang out. I love talking to you. And I swear, I won't even try to kiss you again." She kicks water toward me and says with a laugh, "At least, not tonight."

MAY 19TH

Danny

"HOW'S THE SHOULDER holding up after surgery, Diamond?" Coach asks as I'm leaving the weight room from a preseason training session.

"I'm in the best shape of my life, and for the first time in forever, my shoulder doesn't hurt. This could be our year," I say with a grin.

"You want another ring?"

"Don't you?"

"Hell yeah, I do," he says. "I'm also really appreciative of the guidance you've been giving the rookie. I'm sure it made you nervous when we drafted him."

"I've never been afraid of competition, Coach. You know that. And don't forget, I was the hotshot rookie once, too."

"We've had a good run here together in Kansas City. Add a third ring, and I just might think about retiring. Spend some time with the grandkids. What about you?"

"I'll probably play as long as my body holds out," I tell him. "But it would be good to go out on top. We're going to have a strong offensive unit."

"And the defense is coming together nicely. Hey, have a good trip. You taking any film to study while you're gone?" he asks, but I can tell by the grin on his face that he's joking.

"No way. This vacation is all about relaxation and celebration."

"Good man," Coach says as he heads to his office. "Have a great anniversary trip, and give your wife, Lori, my best."

I walk outside of the practice facility where I'm greeted by numerous fans shouting my name. I sign autographs, shake hands, and take pictures. A small group of beautiful young women is in the mix, waiting until the kids have moved on to the next player to bounce up to me.

"Danny, will you sign my shirt?" one of them asks, pushing her chest out toward me to indicate which part of the shirt she wants signed.

She sexily flips her hair as I take the Sharpie from her and sign closer to her collarbone than her boob.

"I'm Lana," she coos as I sign a football for her equally gorgeous friend. "What are you doing now? Wanna go party with us?"

I know exactly what she's offering.

"Wish I could, ladies, but I have to get home to my wife. We're celebrating our fifteenth anniversary." I'm pretty sure I deserve to be sainted in the afterlife for all the women I've turned down over the years. But, when you have two amazing children and a beautiful wife, it's not worth a few hours of fun. I chuckle to myself. Well, it might be, but I'd never do anything to embarrass my children.

I grab my offensive lineman, a recent divorcé who needs to get back out there. "But you should talk to Randy here. He loves to party."

Randy rolls his eyes at me as I slip away. I know he won't be going anywhere with the girls either but, if nothing else, it's good for his ego.

On the way home, I pick up a bottle of Cristal, a bouquet of flowers, and a pair of custom-made earrings from the jewelers.

Lori, who I sent to the spa to get her out of the house for the day, is going to be so shocked by everything I have planned. Our anniversary was a couple of weeks ago. We went out to dinner with friends and had a great time, but with the kids' school year coming to an end, I knew we wouldn't be able to get away until now. I thought about telling her then but decided to surprise her instead.

WHEN I PULL up to my house, I see there's mass chaos going on as my parents and two children along with the four Mackenzie children and their grandparents are all trying to get loaded into the black SUVs that are taking them to the airport.

"Daddy, you made it in time to say good-bye!" my fourteen-year-old daughter Devaney says, running over to give me a hug.

Since the teen years hit, it's become rare for her to call me Daddy. I take a moment to bask in the glorious sound of it.

"I couldn't miss seeing you off."

"And none of us spilled the beans!" my son, Damon, says. He'll turn thirteen next month, and he is a chip off the old block—always looking for ways to have fun. Fun meaning trouble. "Mom will be so happy!"

The youngest Mackenzie, Madden, who just finished kindergarten, is running around like he's on a sugar rush, knocking over the suitcases. I pick him up. This kid doesn't need sugar. He's got more energy than anyone I've ever met, and he is tough as nails.

"Hey, Crusher, how about we get you buckled in and ready to go? I'll put Ryder next to you," I say, mentioning his nine-year-old brother.

My best friend, Jadyn Mackenzie, smiles thankfully, handing another suitcase to the driver to load in the back as she gives instructions to her oldest son, Chase. He and Damon just finished the seventh grade and both play every sport they can.

"Who do you want to meet most on the Disney cruise?" I ask

Haley James, the second-oldest Mackenzie.

"I'm a little old for all that, don't you think?"

She's eleven going on seventeen and a good athlete herself. Although you'd never know it by looking at her. Right now, she's decked out in a pink satin romper, a furry jacket, and glittery shoes, and she has black sunglasses perched on her head. You'd think she was going to the French Riviera for the Cannes Film Festival, not on a Disney cruise with her grandparents.

"She wants to see the characters from *Frozen*," Chase says, causing Haley to slug him. "You hit like a girl," Chase says, pretending not to be effected even though I see him wince.

But that sets Haley off, and she rushes after him.

"All right!" Jadyn says. "Everyone who wants to go on the cruise with their grandparents needs to get in the car with their backpacks and get buckled up, or you'll be staying home."

All the kids immediately stop screwing around, march over to pick up their packs, and get into the SUVs without a fight.

"Are you sure you're up for this?" she asks the grandparents.

"Of course we are," Mrs. Mackenzie, her mother-in-law, says. "We can handle it."

"We did manage to survive your childhoods on our own," my mother adds.

She's right. Jadyn, her husband, Phillip, and I were best friends growing up in Nebraska and were quite possibly handfuls ourselves.

We do hugs, kisses, and good-byes, and then they take off.

Jadyn sits down on the front step and takes in a deep, cleansing breath. I sit next to her, just like I used to when we were kids.

"Operation Surprise Anniversary Trip has officially commenced. I've gotta be honest," she says. "I didn't know if you and Lori would make it this far. Fifteen years of marriage is a big deal. Congrats."

"Thanks. Our first years were a little rocky, but once we were done having babies, I won my first championship, and I got signed to a long-term contract, things got better. I think she'll be excited about our trip."

"I'm a little nervous she won't love being surprised, but hopefully, she takes it in stride. The kids are sure excited." She leans back and stretches her long legs. "Phillip and I aren't sure what we're going to do with a whole week to ourselves."

I bump her shoulder with mine and grin. "Oh, I'm sure you'll think of *something*. You should go somewhere. Take a trip."

"No way. We travel all the time for work," she says. Jadyn runs a commercial engineering and architectural design firm while Phillip is CEO of a white-glove freight company. "We're going to stay home and enjoy the peace and quiet. Plus, I have a meeting on Wednesday that I can't miss."

"Who would have thought, the girl who skipped her college classes on Fridays to drink all afternoon would turn out to do what you have done? I'm really proud of you, Jay."

"Thanks, Danny. That means a lot coming from a twice-winning Super Bowl champion. Can I borrow your rings, get naked, and try to help Phillip live out a fantasy of his?"

"What fantasy is that?"

"You know he always thought he'd play professional football with you someday. It was both of your dreams, growing up."

"Until he blew out his knee senior year of high school. He's done fine without football. Hell, he's just hitting his stride. I'm getting too old for the game."

"You're only thirty-eight, Danny. That's not old."

"It is for a football player—or so my lovely wife tells me."

"She's just worried about you getting hurt."

"Maybe," I say.

"Are you all ready? Did you pack all her clothes *exactly* like I told you?"

"Yes, I did. I also picked up the champagne and flowers. And these." I pull a box out of my pocket. As much as they cost, I'm not letting them out of my grasp.

Jadyn eyes the store name on the box. "Lori does love jewelry," she says flatly.

"I was thinking I'd give these to her on the plane. Start things off right." I open the box.

"Holy crap! Those had to cost a fortune!"

"Quarter of a million." I shrug. "Fifteen years of putting up with me, she deserves something spectacular, don't you think?"

"You've given her a spectacular life, Danny. She should be giving *you* a gift. Has she even said anything to you about your anniversary? I thought she would throw a fit about just having dinner with friends on the actual date. You usually plan something more extravagant."

"And these earrings are just that. I'm hoping maybe the jewels will loosen up her lips, if you know what I mean."

"You shouldn't have to spend a quarter of a million dollars to get a freaking blow job, Danny," Jadyn says, rolling her eyes. "You're a professional football player. A woman should pay you to allow your championship-winning penis in her mouth."

"Penis? Ugh, I hate that word. Please tell me, when you and Phillip get it on, you don't call it that."

"I'm trying to use the proper terms for the children. I don't want my boys running around, telling people about their dicks. Or worse, using the C-word."

"When did *cock* become a bad word?"

"When your six-year-old screams *big, black cock* over and over at a soccer game." She laughs. "Even if he was referring to the rooster on the shirt you got in the Chianti region of Italy."

"That was fucking funny."

"I wanted to die. Actually, I might have. I'm pretty sure my heart stopped."

"Oh no, don't even joke about that," I tell her, remembering when her heart did stop, and Phillip and I thought we'd lost her. She was in a car accident while pregnant with Chase, which caused a placental abruption, leading to an emergency C-section and her flatlining. Thankfully, they were able to revive her, and both she and the baby survived. I honestly don't know what I would have done without her in my life.

"It's just an expression, Danny," she says, lowering her voice.

I glance at my watch, wondering where my wife is.

"What time is Lori supposed to be home?" Jadyn asks, reading my mind.

"When I sent her to the spa, I told her to be home by five. That I'd made reservations."

"It's almost six. So, she thinks you're going out for dinner?"

"Yeah. She has no idea that I'll be whisking her away on a private jet to Fiji."

A FEW MINUTES later, Lori's sleek Mercedes convertible pulls into our driveway.

She gives Jadyn and me a wave but doesn't come over, so I say, "It's showtime."

Jadyn stands up and gives me a tight hug. "I hope you and Lori have an amazing trip."

What she verbalizes doesn't match her body language, and that worries me.

"Do you think she's going to be mad I sent the kids off and didn't tell her?"

"She's just not big on surprises. You know how she likes to be in control—or at least, have the illusion of control. Maybe give her the earrings first and then tell her about the trip."

"Yeah, maybe you're right."

I walk across the yard, stopping to grab the bottle of champagne and the flowers from the car. When I go inside my house, I notice that my wife looks stressed. Not that you can tell much.

Her face is so Botoxed that she can't really frown. I'm not sure why she is so obsessed with looking young. But then I think back to the girls standing in line for autographs and know the answer. She sees every woman as competition. And I can't fault her for wanting to keep her body perfect for her man.

I step behind her, wrap an arm around her waist, and set the flowers and the champagne on the counter. "You look beautiful," I tell her, knowing she loves hearing it. "How was your day at the spa?"

"It was fine," she says, turning around to face me. "Are the kids next door?"

"Before we talk about that," I say, flashing my endorsement-winning smile, "I want to give you this. I know we didn't do much on our actual anniversary, but there was a reason for that." I pull the box from my pocket and place it in her hand.

"Oh, Danny!" she exclaims. "You shouldn't have!"

"Here, let me," I suggest, opening the box and exposing the dazzling diamonds. "Danny Diamond's wife of fifteen years deserves some spectacular diamonds, don't you think?"

The sparkling stones reflect in Lori's eyes and give me hope that this week will be perfect. Lori's been a little distant lately. Not that it's uncommon. She goes through phases, I guess you'd say. Sometimes, our sex life is amazing. Other times, it's practically nonexistent. It all depends on her moods and how she's feeling about herself. About three years ago, after she got her boob job and tummy tuck, she was hot for me all the time. As we both approach our fortieth birthdays, she pretty much has her plastic surgeon on speed dial. All the Botox, nips, and tucks are expensive, but it's worth it. You know what they say; *happy wife, happy life.* In my case, that's very true. When Lori's happy, she keeps me happy in bed. And that makes me happy. This vacation is exactly what we need to reconnect and get back on track.

"Danny, these are gorgeous!" She slips off the large diamond studs I got her a few years ago and replaces them with the new chandelier earrings. "They must have cost a fortune!"

"I can afford it," I say.

"*We* can afford it, you mean," she snaps back.

"Of course that's what I meant. Fifteen years is a big deal. You're a big deal. You deserve them."

I pop the bottle of champagne and pour us each a glass while she pulls a mirror from her purse to check out the earrings. I consider drinking straight from the bottle like we used to when we were first married, wondering if she'd like it. But I know I should behave. Lori prefers sophistication and propriety these days. I hand her a flute and graciously raise mine in a toast.

"Here's to you and to fifteen more years of happiness."

She doesn't say anything in response. I think she's too overwhelmed by the earrings to speak.

"I have more surprises. Wait here."

"Danny—" she starts to say, but I cut her off. I'm excited to tell her the rest.

I run around the corner and pull our already packed suitcases out to the kitchen.

"What's going on?"

"You and I are going to Fiji. And we're leaving, well, now. I have everything planned. Everything you could possibly need is packed. And the kids just left for a Disney cruise with my parents. I wanted us to have a second honeymoon."

"Danny," she says.

And I'm not sure why, but I get the feeling I'm going to be in trouble.

"Yeah?" I ask, hoping she's okay that I planned this. Hoping she doesn't want to open the suitcase and go through everything before we leave. Hoping she'll be the carefree woman I met and fell in love with.

"This isn't what I signed up for."

"What do you mean?"

"A husband who models underwear, who—"

"Thanks to those underwear ads and all my endorsements, I could afford to splurge on those earrings."

"And who has women with signs asking him to marry them."

"Babe, it just goes with the territory of being married to a professional football player. You were excited when I got drafted, and we've been so fortunate to be able to stay in Kansas City. So many of my friends are constantly uprooting their families for a different team."

"I would have loved to go somewhere a little more glamorous," she says. That's always been a bone of contention with her. She wanted me to get traded. Thought I could earn more. "Regardless, I honestly didn't think you'd still be playing at this stage in our life."

"What did you think?"

"That you'd play for a few years and then get a normal job."

"A normal job couldn't have bought you those earrings."

"I have to admit, I was excited when you hurt your shoulder. I thought it would force you to retire."

"Why would I have done that? I'm back and better than ever."

"Yes," she says with an irritated sigh, "so you've told me."

"What's wrong? Why do you seem pissed? I've spent hours planning this trip. Planned the spa day, so you wouldn't know the kids were leaving, set up the cruise, got my parents to take them, helped them pack, chartered a private jet, had the earrings custom-made. They cost a quarter of a million dollars, Lori."

"Maybe you should have bought another Ferrari, Danny."

I roll my eyes. *Really?* She's bringing up the Ferrari I bought with my signing bonus when I first got drafted after a wild night in Vegas for Phillip's bachelor party. She's always hated that car.

"Can we not do this now? Can we just go have some fun?" I plead.

"I can't go to Fiji with you."

"Why not?"

"Because I don't want to be married to you."

I take a step back, wondering if I heard her right. "What? Are you serious?"

"Yes, I'm serious. Actually, this works out better than I planned. It'll allow me to move out while the kids are gone. We can break the news to them when they get home."

"Move out? But where will you go?" I ask, dumbfounded.

"I'm seeing someone, Danny. I'm moving in with him."

I instantly feel like I was sacked. A vicious, blindside hit. A hit so hard, I can feel it in my teeth because it rattles my bones, hits nerves, and sends aftershocks through my body, even before I hit the ground.

"*Seeing*? As in you've been having an *affair*?"

"Technically, I suppose you could call it that," she says flatly.

"In other words, you've been fucking another guy while you are married to me?" My disbelief in her wanting to leave me turns to outright rage.

"Yes."

"Who?" *I'm going to kill him.*

"Dr. Rash."

"Your plastic surgeon?"

"Yeah."

"So, all the appointments you've had for your boobs, the tucks, the lifts, the facials, the Botox—"

"That's how we met."

"You've got to be kidding me. I've been paying him to screw my wife?"

"Danny, look, it's not working. I'm not happy. You'll be fine. You have plenty of women who want you." She doesn't look me in the eye when she says this; in fact, she's looking at her freshly manicured nails, like we're discussing the weather and not our relationship.

"How long?"

"How long what?" she asks, finally looking up.

"How long have you been sleeping with him?"

"Oh." She shrugs. "About a year."

A horn honks out front, causing her to plaster a fake smile on her face. "Richard is here. Sorry, but I have to go." She gives me an air kiss, grabs the suitcase I packed full of new clothes, bikinis, and sexy lingerie, and walks out the front door. *Our* front door.

I drop to a chair in my living room and sit in stunned silence, wondering what the heck just happened.

And then I realize that she left, wearing the earrings.

OCTOBER 25TH

Jennifer

I'M HAVING A shitty day. No, it's worse than shitty. Paparazzi are camped outside my house, hoping to catch a glimpse of me, hoping to see me looking as ragged as I feel. I'm just hoping, if I stay here long enough, they'll forget about me and move on. Find their next scandal.

My phone dings for the millionth time. I seriously don't know how they got my cell number but, this time, as I glance at it, a familiar name pop up.

Mama: *I'm pretty sure I told you so…*

Me: *Actually, you didn't. You said that, if we weren't married in the church, our relationship wouldn't count. Yet we were together for over a decade.*

Mama: *A churchgoing man wouldn't have done what he did. He's not only off the wagon; he's off the plantation. Color me not surprised.*

Me: *Well, I am. And it hurts.*

Mama: *Once an alcoholic, always an alcoholic. I told you that, too. He's just like your no-good daddy.*

Me: *Thanks for your support. It means a lot.*

Mama: *Don't get all snippy with me, young lady. I called* *and called, but you didn't answer, so I had to resort to this newfangled texting. I just want to say that you're always welcome at home.*

Me: *Thank you, Mama. I'll think about it.*

No way in hell am I going home. My parents live across the street from each other, and even though they were married in a church, they are about as dysfunctional as they come. They won't get a divorce because of their religious beliefs. Daddy started drinking again when I was six, and Mama kicked him out. To annoy her, he moved into the house across the street. Since then, they've lived to spite each other. It's part of why I've never married. I don't ever want to be like them. I also swore, I'd never be in a relationship with someone who couldn't control their drinking.

But here I am.

Mama was right about one thing though. I do need to get out of town.

As I'm contemplating where to go, another text pops up on my screen. I glance at it, assuming it's Mama needing to get the last word in even if only by text.

Instead, I see it's from an unknown number. I click over, intending to delete it, but the preview makes me curious, so I click on the full message.

You might not remember me, and this might not even still be your number, but this is Jadyn Mackenzie. We met at a Nebraska game a long time ago. If this is Jennifer Edwards, first of all, I'm really sorry for everything you're going through. It must be awful. Second of all, this sounds crazy, but if you need to get out of LA, you are welcome to come stay with us in Kansas City. Not too many paparazzi there.

My heart does a flip as my mind flits back. It's been, what? Fourteen years since I met a handsome, charismatic rookie quarterback named Danny Diamond? We had a crazy, instant connection. The kind of connection that, if he hadn't been a newlywed with a brand-new baby, I would have acted upon that night.

I reply to Jadyn. I don't know why. Maybe because I'm a glutton for punishment. I've followed Danny's career. I was in the stands when he won his first Championship. I obsessed over the photo of him holding his adorable little girl as confetti rained down on them that went viral and caused ovaries around the world to simultaneously explode. I understood why he stopped talking to me, why he chose to focus on his family, even though things were rocky with his wife. Or maybe it's because Danny made me feel different—an odd combination of being extremely turned on while visions of a future together danced through my head like sugarplums. It sounds unbelievable, but on the night Danny and I met, I knew he was my future. I could see it all. Cheering for him at his games, having kids together, growing old.

We decided to just be friends though, and I respected him for being faithful to his wife.

I went to a Nebraska football game. By some miracle, he ended up there without his wife. I met his friends and loved them. We had so much fun together even though things were kept completely platonic.

I close my eyes, remembering how I felt when I saw the text from him saying he couldn't see or talk to me again. There were other things said, but they didn't matter. The damage was done. My heart felt shattered.

But then I met Troy at a friend's wedding not long after, and we've pretty much been together ever since.

Well, *were* together.

And the last thing I need is to be on the other side of a tabloid scandal. I can only imagine the headlines if I had an affair with Danny. Although it would be the perfect place to get away, and I'm dying to see him again, I can't.

I just can't.

Not to mention the fact that I haven't seen these people in years and, even then, I only spent a short time with them. I know she's sincere though. Jadyn is one of Danny's best friends and was one of the most honest and real people I've ever met.

> **Me:** *It's great to hear from you. And thank you. I really appreciate the offer, but I'm not sure Danny's wife would like it.*
>
> **Jadyn:** *Remember when we were at the Nebraska game, and we talked briefly about fate? About people coming into your life for a reason? Maybe today is that reason. I'll warn you in advance though. We have four kids and a dog, and sometimes, our house can be a little chaotic.*
>
> **Jadyn:** *Okay, I lied. It's always chaotic.*

I'm getting ready to say, *Thanks, but no, thanks,* when another text pops up.

> **Troy:** *Baby, I'm so sorry. I promise I'll go back to rehab.*

I hear a car pull into the driveway, shouts from reporters, and the clicking of high-speed lenses. A few moments later, Troy comes in the front door with his manager, Jason, tagging along behind him. Troy looks horrible. Like he's been to hell and somehow clawed his way back.

"What are you doing here?" I ask, trying to remain unaffected by him.

"I need to set things right with you."

Somehow, I knew that's what he was going to say. It's what he *always* says.

"I told you not to come home. How can you even think of stepping foot in this house after what you did? You humiliated me—no, you humiliated yourself."

"I know, I know." He takes two strides toward me and slides his hand into the back of my hair. What used to be comforting now feels foreign. He looks deep into my eyes. "I had champagne backstage. You know I can handle a few glasses, but then I don't know what happened. Things spiraled out of control. I didn't mean to do it. Those girls meant nothing to me. I barely even remember what happened."

"I told you this on the phone, but I'll say it again in person," I say, backing away from him. "We. Are. Through."

"Don't say that, Eddy," he says, using his nickname for me. "I love you. You're just mad. You can't throw away our life together."

"Troy, *you* are the one who threw our life away. I had nothing to do with it. I've stood by you every time something like this happened. You might not remember, but I do. I literally pulled you out of the gutter because the people you were partying with didn't give a shit and left you there to die. And I got a black eye for my efforts. But I stood by you. Got you into rehab. A few years later, you called me drunk—again—from an alley because the prostitute you'd been with robbed you. I told you, when you went to rehab the second time, I wouldn't be around if there were ever a need for a third."

"I came back home because we're going to work it out." He's sweating and crying and miserable. I can't stand it. And I refuse to let it affect me. "I'm not leaving."

"Fine," I say, pivoting on my heel. I grab my purse and make my way toward the garage door.

"You can't go!" he yells, coming at me.

I'm instantly scared. It wouldn't be the first time he lashed out at me in a fit of rage, but usually, he was drunk. Now that I study him closer, I realize he might be just that.

Fortunately, his manager grabs him from behind. "Let her go, man."

I take one last look at Troy, broken and pathetic. Certainly not the larger-than-life rock star I first fell for. When I shut the door behind me, I know I'm closing it on a big chapter of my life.

I get in the car, throw on a pair of dark sunglasses, and wonder where I'm going. The second I open the garage door, the press will surround me. When I pull away, they will follow.

Jadyn didn't say anything about Danny's wife. But it doesn't matter. If I go to Kansas City, it won't be because of him.

I think back to my earlier phone conversation with one of Troy's friends, who called me as soon as the news broke. Who told me I should hear Troy's side of the story before I jumped to any conclusions. That I should give him a chance to explain. That maybe we needed religious counseling this time. There's no way in the world he could explain away the video images of his alcohol-and-drug-induced orgy at an Amsterdam brothel. I'll never be able to unsee the things he did with those women. And I'll never be able to unhear his answer when one of the girls asked about the *Eddy* tattoo on his arm. She thought it was about a guy and that he went both ways.

What he should have said was that the tattoo was the nickname he called the woman he loved, but instead, he said, "She's nobody."

Tears fill my eyes. Part of me wants to run back in there. To make it all better. I want to forget what I saw. I want us to work. I want him to love me. I want him to get better. To be the kind of man worthy of my love. The man I thought he could be.

But I can't. For myself. I can't do this anymore.

What I need is a no-bullshit friend.

So, I reply.

Me: *Probably a different kind of chaos than what I'm* *facing here. Is it crazy that I'm considering taking you up on your offer?*

Jadyn: *Not at all crazy. I have a meeting in Santa Monica first thing tomorrow morning. You could meet me at the airport around 9:30 a.m. and fly home with me on the corporate jet.*

Me: *Are you in town now?*

Jadyn: *Yep. Just finished up for the day. I'm sitting at the hotel bar, having a well-deserved glass of wine.*

Me: *If I do this, I have to figure out a way to ditch the paparazzi. Going to a hotel, spending the night, and leaving with you in the morning might be ideal. And I could really use some wine.*

Jadyn: *I'd love the company.*

She texts me where she's staying. It's an iconic Beverly Hills hotel on Rodeo Drive. I was there for an event a few years ago and probably would not choose to stay there. It looked like it'd seen better days.

Regardless, I pick up my phone and call my assistant.

"Jennifer, how are you?" she asks by way of greeting.

"As well as can be expected, Sarah. I need you to do me a favor." I proceed to give her the specifics.

When I end the call, I hit the door opener, causing the California sun to stream in and light up the dark garage. Like a new day dawning. A symbol of me starting over. I take a deep breath, back out of the driveway, and pretend not to notice the cameras.

A few of the more enthusiastic photographers follow me in their cars. The traffic in LA is terrible, and it takes what feels like forever to get from Malibu to the hotel.

When I pull up, the photographers don't follow. They know better than to trespass here. When the valet opens the door and I step out, I suddenly realize how I'm dressed. I look down at the slippers on my feet. The dirty white T-shirt I've been wearing for three days. I didn't even look in the mirror this morning. I couldn't bear to. Now, I wish I had.

I start laughing at myself. It's either that or start crying.

"Miss Edwards," the valet says gently, obviously knowing that I'm quite possibly going to have a mental breakdown right here in the drive, "do you have a bag?"

"No."

"I understand your assistant will be retrieving your car tomorrow."

"Yes, that's correct."

"Very well. If you would allow me, I'd be happy to take you through the back entrance and straight to your room."

"I look too rough to go through the lobby?" I laugh again. You'd think I was the one who had been on a bender. *This is absurd.*

"For what it's worth," he says as I follow him through the underbelly of the hotel and up a service elevator, "I'm sorry for what you're going through. If there's anything we can do, please let the staff know."

"Thank you. I will."

I text Jadyn.

Me: *I'm here at the hotel. My assistant booked me a room. Troy showed up at home, so I just grabbed my purse. This is a little embarrassing, but when I got here, I realized that I wasn't dressed appropriately, and I didn't bring any clothes.*

Jadyn: *How about I grab a bottle of wine from the bar and come up there?*

That's exactly what I need. A bottle of wine and a good cry.

A few minutes later, there's a knock at my door. I look out the peephole and can't help but smile. Jadyn looks just the same. I'd recognize her anywhere.

I throw open the door.

"You look amazing," I tell her.

She's dressed so differently than the last time I saw her when she was in jeans and a tight-fitting Nebraska T-shirt, but even in the expensive tailored suit, there's an underlying casualness about her. Her face is still girlish, her skin glowing and healthy, her hair still long and blonde, and her body still thin and shapely.

"And you don't," she says, taking in my disheveled state, quickly setting the bottle on the closest flat surface, and then wrapping me in a hug.

I didn't expect the hug. It feels warm and motherly and wonderful. I start crying.

"It's okay," she says. "Get it all out, and then tell me about it. I can't believe he just showed up at your house."

I stand in the hallway of my suite, the door not even shut behind us, and cry on the shoulder of someone I barely know. I'm pretty sure I'm not the only one who just hit rock bottom.

EVENTUALLY, I STOP bawling, pull myself together, and invite Jadyn to sit down. "Fill me in on what's going on with you all."

"No," she says sternly. "First, you are going to go shower." She rummages through a large designer tote and pulls out a bag. "Then, put on a little of this makeup. While you do that, I'm going to run out and get you some things to wear."

I study the older Jadyn. "Danny told me you weren't the typical girlie girl. That you didn't like to shop."

"I have four kids to feed, clothe, and care for. My job involves designing and purchasing construction materials and furnishings for entire buildings. Shopping is pretty much my life now." She gives me a smirk. "But, trust me, I am not a wander-around kind of shopper. I go to the right store, get exactly what I need, and am out the door. If I can't find anything for you to wear on Rodeo

Drive, something is wrong with me. I'll be back before you know it."

I consider telling her the name of a shop I frequent. They know my sizes and could whip together a wardrobe, but I'll be going to Kansas City, and I figure she knows what style would suit me better there.

She gives me another hug, turns me around, walks me into the bathroom, cranks on the shower, and walks out.

It makes me feel like crying again. This is what a real friend does.

As I pour body wash into my hand, I do start crying, feeling sorry for myself.

I traveled with Troy whenever my filming schedule allowed it, but I tried to always go on tour with him, as that was when he was most likely to relapse. One of my best friends stood by me the first time Troy needed rehab, but the second time, she told me that, unless he changed his lifestyle, too, I was going to live my entire life this way. She knew I wanted kids and said that they shouldn't be brought into that kind of world. Her father was an alcoholic, like mine, and she had suffered from it. I thought she was taking out her past on me, not looking at my situation. But she knew better than I did. When I didn't listen, we grew apart. I did a lot of things in the name of love that I shouldn't have. I made excuses to myself, excuses for him.

As the warm water washes over me, I have a renewed sense of well-being. I deserve better. I deserve to be better to myself.

This epiphany causes me to stop crying and get serious about making myself presentable and, although I'm going through the motions of making myself look better from an outward standpoint, internally, I am being real. I just turned thirty-six. My internal clock has been ticking for a while. I've set aside my dreams for someone else's—or maybe I didn't want to bring a child into my relationship with Troy. Maybe I knew something deep down that I wasn't willing to admit. That, eventually, we'd end like this. Crashed and burned in a wreckage filled with drugs, booze, and an Amsterdam brothel.

Okay, I never thought a brothel would be involved, but whatever.

I think about what I want out of life. What I've *always* wanted out of life. A man who loves me unconditionally, who wants to marry me, who wants that commitment. A man who wants a baby with me—but then I stop myself. This is bullshit. I don't need a man. I have me. If I want a family, I can make my own, either through adoption or donor sperm.

Maybe staying with Jadyn is exactly what I need. To see how life works for a normal family. How they balance time with their kids, with their jobs, and with each other. Maybe it will show me that I can do it, too.

Troy and I always kept our money separate—thank goodness. Fortunately, he slightly outearns me, so even though my mother always reminds me that he's my common-law husband, the state of California does not recognize such unions. Even the house we live in is owned by him. He purchased it right before we got together. Now that I think about it, that's probably why he showed up there. His manager, Jason, was worried I'd change the locks and try to stake a claim to it.

What this all means is that our long relationship can end immediately. No messy divorce. No fighting about dividing up assets. All I need to do is send movers to pick up my clothes and personal belongings. I smile. Actually, I'll make Jason set it up. I grab my phone and make the call.

"Jason, it's me," I say when he answers. "Please don't tell Troy I'm calling. I don't want to upset him further. I assume you had him come home because you were worried I'd try to take the house from him."

"Hang on," he says to me. I hear him say to Troy, "I need to take this outside."

A few moments later, he comes back on the line. "I was concerned about it, yes. After what he did, most women would be feeling pretty, uh, spiteful."

"You might not know the details of our finances, but we have nothing held jointly. The house is in his name, and we never commingled assets. I was wondering if you would be willing to hire someone to pack up my personal effects—clothes, jewelry, photos, the stuff in my office along with my Jeep, which is still in the garage—and have them sent to my storage unit until I find a place to live."

"You're really not going to sue him?"

"I just want it to be over. It's just over," I say with resolve.

"I understand," he says, "and I will take care of that for you. For whatever it's worth, I'm sorry this happened."

"Sorry it happened or sorry he got caught?"

"Sorry it happened. I knew he drank the champagne, which had been happening more and more lately. But he came back to the hotel with me and said he was going to bed. I immediately passed out. With the flights and time changes, we hadn't slept in nearly thirty-six hours. Obviously, he had something besides the champagne because he should have been dead on his feet like me. I had no idea he would drink more in his room and then go out."

"Sounds like Troy," I say with a sigh. "Jason, take care of him, okay?"

"I will. Bye."

I cry again. But the bout is shorter, and by the time Jadyn returns, I'm looking and feeling more like myself. She's followed into the room by a bellman, who has a trolley filled with shopping bags and a single suitcase as well as a rolling clothing rack.

"You moving in?" I ask with a laugh, seeing the suitcase and assuming my suite is probably nicer than her room.

"No, everything I bought should fit into that suitcase. I figured you wouldn't want to schlep all these shopping bags around."

She tips the bellman handsomely, based on his profuse thanks, and he departs.

"You really got me a whole wardrobe in under two hours?"

"Yes, I did. And you look much better."

There is a knock on the door.

"That was fast," she says, opening the door.

A steward brings in a tray full of decadent-looking desserts, including a pint of my favorite ice cream, and a chilled bottle of champagne.

I pick up the ice cream. "I don't think this is on the menu."

"It's not." She smiles. "But it's what you got when we stopped at the convenience store after the football game. Before we went to the hayrack ride. Do you remember that?"

Tears start to fill my eyes again—not for Troy this time, but because of the one who got away.

"I was so enamored with Danny. I didn't care that he was married. I admit, it was selfish of me, and one of my biggest regrets is not pursuing him further. But he was so sincere when he told me he couldn't even be my friend. I was heartbroken. I truly thought I had found my soul mate."

"I thought you had, too," she says, handing me a spoon. "I felt really torn about his decision. On one hand, I was proud of him for being responsible, for not giving up on his marriage, and for making his baby a priority. On the other hand, my heart ached because I wanted him to be crazy, happy in love."

"I'm surprised you'd say that. Aren't you and his wife best friends? Do you still live next door to each other?"

"To answer the question of if we are friends, I'd have to go back to the beginning."

She grabs a chocolate truffle, pops it into her mouth, and then opens the champagne, pouring us each a glass.

As I'm trying to come up with something to say that effectively sums up my gratitude for what she's done, she says simply and graciously, "To renewed friendships."

Simple, to the point.

I'm glad now that I couldn't come up with anything because I tend to overtalk. Word-vomiting comes to mind. When I won my first Academy Award, I announced to the press that I'd had a few shots. I kissed everyone at the after-party. I realize I've gone from the girl who always bluntly blurted out the truth to a woman who's afraid of the truth.

Jadyn starts pulling items out of bags and arranges them on the rolling rack.

"Why don't you try on clothes while I catch you up?"

She studies me as she hands me the first outfit. I notice it came from four different stores.

"Here's the deal though," she says. "If I'm going to catch you up, you have to catch me up on your life, too. And no bullshit fairy-tale version. Stuff like what happened in Amsterdam doesn't usually just happen randomly. There had to have been signs."

"There were," I admit. I take a swig of champagne, shove a spoonful of ice cream into my mouth, and take the clothes into the bathroom.

I come back out, wearing a bra and underwear that fit perfectly, a pair of red velvet skinny jeans, designer booties, and a black graphic tee that says, *No Photos Please*, along with an Alice + Olivia patched jean jacket. I can't help but laugh at her sense of humor.

"It all fits perfectly," I say in amazement. I usually try on a million pairs of jeans to find one that fits.

"This kind of thing is my everyday wardrobe," she says. "Comfortable but pulled together. And you can mix the jeans with these two tops." She takes out another long-sleeved shirt and a lightweight sweater along with a Burberry scarf that matches the jeans and a cute pair of loafers. "Fall in the Midwest can be a challenge. It's chilly when you wake up in the morning, but by midday, it's warm, so layers are key. I got you this brown leather jacket, too. It will go with everything. It seems like, whenever I saw you in the tabloids, you had on black, so I figured you might be ready for a change, something softer."

"A softer freaking life," I blurt out, my old habits coming back.

Jadyn raises her eyebrows and lets out a laugh. "Finally! The Jennifer I know and love! It's good to have you back!"

"Based on this outfit, I don't think I need to try on the rest," I say, peeking through the clothes.

There is a small handbag, an evening clutch, and a tote. All brands I love but styles I haven't chosen in years.

When did I change? When did I morph into what I've become? When did I go from casual, crazy Jennifer Edwards to this shell of her?

I dig through the bags, finding undergarments, pajamas and a robe, four different yoga outfits—the kind you look good in at the gym or on the street—a couple of daytime dresses, a few pairs of jeans, a bunch of shirts and scarfs, a pair of dress slacks, a plaid blazer, two skirts, and four pairs of shoes that somehow manage to go with it all.

"This is amazing," I tell her. "Really, thank you." I stop speaking when I notice a garment bag draped over the back of a chair. "What's that?"

"I'd like to leave that one wrapped up, if you don't mind."

"Why?"

"It's a dress. One that I hope you will eventually need. But I don't want to get ahead of myself."

"Let's go out," I suddenly say.

"Where do you want to go?"

"Somewhere to be seen. To prove I'm okay," I reply confidently, getting myself mentally geared up.

I'll flip off the paparazzi. Show them I'm fine.

"Prove to whom?" she asks.

What she says stops me in my tracks. "Everyone," I mutter.

The minute it tumbles out of my mouth, I understand.

The Jennifer she knew wouldn't have cared what anyone thought. She was a rebel in Hollywood. She took selfies on the red carpet and openly fangirled. Her award acceptance speeches were routinely bleeped. She would get onstage, be handed an award, and say, "I'm so effing shocked I'm even up here, I don't know what to say."

"You're right. I have nothing to prove, and I'm pretty sure I haven't eaten in a couple of days."

"The bar downstairs where I was when you texted is supposed to have good food. I planned to have dinner there."

"Gosh, there you were, enjoying a nice glass of wine after a hard day, and I interrupted all that. You're probably hungry."

"That I am." She grabs the desserts from the table, thoughtfully putting them in the mini fridge, and then says, "Let's go."

We head downstairs to the hotel's wood-paneled bar and quickly order a bottle of red along with a couple of Kansas City strips. I take that as a positive sign. In most restaurants here, they call them *New York* strips.

"You seem better," Jadyn says.

"I am. Not just better than I was because of what had happened, but also because I realize that my relationship with Troy caused me to change. I miss me. But I don't want to talk about that. Tell me about you! About your family. Show me a million pictures!"

She grabs her phone and pulls up a photo of a tall, cute boy. "This is Chase, our oldest."

"He looks just like you."

"He does, but his personality is all Phillip. He's mature, poised, and smart."

"How old is he?"

"Almost fourteen. He's an eighth grader this year."

"Fourteen? He has muscles. And how tall is he?"

"Six foot. He's really into sports, and he works out a lot." She scrolls to another pic. "Our daughter, Haley James. She's eleven. Total tomboy, like I was, but dresses like a girlie girl and cheers competitively."

"She's beautiful," I say. "And she looks like trouble."

Jadyn laughs. "I think she and Danny's son, Damon, might give us a run for our money. Paybacks for the trouble we got into when we were young."

When she says Danny's name, my heart skips a beat, but I hold my tongue and don't ask about him. I need to be polite and get caught up with her first.

She scrolls to another photo of two little boys. "Ryder and Madden are nine and six."

"They are adorable. Such a mix of you and Phillip."

"They are each amazing in their own way. It's so crazy how, with hot sex and some genetic mixing, you have this little human. They look related, but it's just weird how they have such distinct personalities and looks." She gets a big smile on her face. "Here's one of Phillip and Danny out on the boat recently."

I examine this photo a little closer. Both guys are shirtless and still quite droolworthy. A flashback of that kiss on the beach floods my thoughts. That's how I have always referred to it—*that kiss*. The only kiss in my life that has ever mattered.

"Juggling a family and two busy careers is definitely challenging," Jadyn says, leading me to believe I must have asked her something in my Danny-memories-induced haze. "But we make it work. We've been creative, and it's why we splurged on the plane."

"The corporate plane? It's, like, yours?"

"Technically, the ownership is split between my company and Phillip's. We were spending way too much time in airports. And there was a tax thing that allowed us to write off a large portion of it, so the timing was right. It's helped immensely."

"When we met, you were working for Phillip and designing a building or something, right?"

"Yes, and now, I own a commercial engineering and architectural design firm that does work all over the country. I sort of specialize in corporate headquarters but, recently, I did a small call center. The owner of that company was so impressed, he asked me to redesign his hotel chain. Hotels were something I'd never tackled before, so I agreed to do one and see how it goes. That's why I'm in town."

"Wow, so you've done well."

"Yeah, I guess."

"And Phillip's company?"

"Still white-glove deliveries, which is booming due to both internet shopping and the fact that Phillip could sell ice to an Eskimo."

"Well, he is pretty cute," I say. "That never hurts."

"Initially, that was true. But he's built a great sales team. His dad retired a couple of years ago, making Phillip the CEO, so he doesn't sell much anymore."

The appetizers are delivered to our table.

"Can I get a shot?" I ask the waiter.

"Sure. What would you like?"

"Do you want one?" I ask Jadyn.

"Of course."

"Bring us something strong but that doesn't taste like alcohol," I request. Then I start chowing down on the food, suddenly ravenous. Both for good food and a good life. I can't wait to get out and start living my life again. That makes me blurt out, "Do you know anyone who has kids that did it themselves?"

"Like a single mom?" Jadyn asks. "Of course. I try to hire moms in my business whenever I can. Moms get work done fast."

"And they do okay? Like, their kids turn out okay?"

She studies me. "Did Troy not want children?"

"He said we were too busy. Traveled too much. It was a subject of contention between us, but I never pushed it. My father was an alcoholic." I lower my voice a notch. "So is Troy. He's always struggled with sobriety, and what you've seen in the tabloids was the result of a binge."

"Motherhood is amazing," she says. "Whether you have them yourself or adopt. Our friends Katie and Neil have two biological children and two who are adopted. You'll get to meet them on Sunday. We're having a big get-together at our house."

"That's soon. Are you ready?"

She stifles a laugh. "Most of our entertaining is pretty casual. Everyone brings food. It's about hanging out, not creating the perfect party."

"That's amazing." I'm ready to ask about Danny when the waiter brings the shots, interrupting our conversation.

"Lemon drop shots with sugared lemons, made with citron and regular vodka," he says. "Technically, a double shot."

"Perfect," I say, quickly slamming it down before I notice that Jadyn has her glass in the air.

I'm an idiot.

"If you're going to hang out with us," she says, "you'll have to get used to the fact that we toast all the time. It's Danny's fault really. When he, Phillip, and I drank our first beers in eighth grade, he toasted to the good life. We've been toasting to our good lives ever since."

"Has Danny's life been good?" I blurt out.

"Yes, and no," she says.

And it gives me hope. For what, I'm not sure.

"Danny is an optimist. To be a good quarterback, he has to be. For example, when he threw an interception or an opposing team cheered loudly, he always pretended—" She laughs. "Actually, knowing his ego, he probably *actually believed* they were cheering for him. It's why he's so levelheaded on the playing field.

Things are not as bad as they seem, and he can overcome it. He's a hard worker, and he gives his all to everything he does in life. Always has."

"I've seen his underwear ads. So, is his life as perfect as his body?"

"No one's life is perfect, Jennifer," she replies.

I nod and toss another shrimp in my mouth, hoping she'll continue.

"My parents passed away at the end of my senior year in high school, and I was determined to live life to the fullest—probably going a little overboard in that regard. I dated a lot. Partied a lot. Had a good time. Because of Danny and Phillip, I hung out with a lot of guys.

"Lori was in my sorority, but we weren't friends at first. She acted like she was above it all. I always wondered why she even rushed. But a few years passed. She loosened up a little, and we became sort of unlikely friends.

"I introduced her to Danny at a party, but she wouldn't give him the time of day. She wanted to get her medical degree and marry a doctor. No room in her life plan for a cocky jock. She knew zero about football, and even though he was like a campus god, she didn't care. I literally had to bribe her just to go on a date with Danny. He liked her because she was pretty and smart, and she *wasn't* impressed that he was an athlete.

"They fell in love and dated for a year. He got drafted, and they were engaged and married within a couple of months. A few months after that, she was pregnant. Phillip and I got married and pregnant not long after, and our babies were born just five months apart …"

"It feels like you're about to say, *but then* …"

"That's because I am. *But then* things started changing. Her not going to medical school was big though. Supposedly, it was her lifelong dream, but she gave up her spot the second she got married. Then she had a rough pregnancy. I felt bad for her, but she also seemed to use it as an excuse for just being kind of bitchy. Toward the end of her pregnancy, some photos of Danny and me together were leaked in the press. The photos showed us having lunch, shopping together at a jewelry store, and then checking into a hotel. I had helped him plan a special night for her. I had a million candles in my bag, and he had bought her a spectacular piece of jewelry. Granted, based on the photos and if you didn't know us, you might think something was going on, but she should have known better. And I get that she was hormonal and irrational, but she went ballistic and said some horrible things to both of us. It was a mess. I thought they might break up before the baby was even born.

"They made up and had the baby, and life seemed okay. Well, not really. She was a wreck after the baby, too. And she wouldn't let Danny help. Got mad if he did something she thought was wrong even though she had no clue what she was doing. A few months after the baby was born, Danny was miserable. His wife was wound up tight and constantly on edge. He talked her into a date night, and Phillip and I watched Devaney."

"That's such a cool name," I interrupt.

"Danny came up with it. I was impressed."

"After a former coach, right? I think I read that in an interview about the photo of Danny and his daughter after his team won the world championship game."

"Wasn't that the best photo ever? So much raw emotion," she gushes. "I blew it up and framed it for him. And I have a smaller version of it in my office." She pauses and takes a bite of shrimp, chews, pats her lips with a napkin, and continues, "Anyway, they had a great night out, and when they came to pick up the baby, I was hopeful that things would be better between them. But then Lori got pissed because, while they were out, we'd run out of breast milk. I had gone to their house, but there was no extra, so we gave the baby a little formula. I was pregnant and knew I wanted to nurse, but I had read up on it and knew, on occasion, it was fine to mix formula into the baby's diet. And it was sort of an emergency. The baby was hungry. And she was colicky and didn't sleep much. Turns out, she was allergic to something Lori had been eating, and that's why her tummy always hurt, and she wouldn't sleep; that is what led them to figuring it out. Regardless, Lori got crazy upset, started yelling at me, and told me I would be a terrible mother."

I see the hurt in Jadyn's eyes, even now, years later. It makes me want to punch Lori in the face.

"Phillip basically kicked her out of our house," she says, practically swooning at the thought.

That's what I want. A guy who will protect me. Who will stand up for me.

"She and Danny got into a huge fight, and he didn't go home that night. I thought it might be over. But they made up again. Even though she didn't work outside the home, Danny hired a nanny and a housekeeper to help her. I'd like to say that she became less of a bitch, but that's not true. She became an entitled bitch, but thankfully, she bitched less at Danny, which made him happier." She takes a sip of water. "I feel like I'm doing all the talking. I don't intend to tell you their life story, but it's important that you understand where Danny's been, so you can understand where he is now."

"Keep going," I say with a nod because I want to know every single shred of detail about Danny's life.

I want to hear I made the right decision back then, that it all worked out and that he's deliriously happy now. Because he deserves it. But, if I'm being honest, there's a big part of me that wishes he were miserable. That he would divorce his wife, so he could live happily ever after with me.

Jadyn's phone vibrates on the table. "I'm sorry. It's my family.

We video chat before bed." She glances at her watch. "As usual, Phillip has let them sweet-talk him into staying up too late. Do you mind?"

"Not at all."

I watch as she answers. We're sitting close in a booth meant for lovers, so I can see her screen. Her children are adorable.

They all yell, "Hi, Mommy," over the top of each other, the youngest jumping up into the screen.

"It's late there. You should all be in bed," she scolds.

"Daddy and Uncle Danny took us out for pizza and beer!" her daughter says. "We played video games for hours. And I beat Damon at air hockey!"

She throws her arm up in a fist pump and hits one of the boys in the head. When he punches her back, she just grins.

"But we had to do our homework before we went," Chase, the oldest says, clearly sticking up for his dad.

"I'm glad you had a fun night. Now, get to bed. Sweet dreams. I love you."

There is a chorus of, "I love you."

She smiles at her children, her love for them apparent, but when Phillip's face comes on the screen, that look changes to something different—desire mixed with deep love. Their chemistry is still as off the charts as I remember.

The way it was with me and Danny.

"You're in trouble for keeping them out so late," she says, but it's clear she's not really mad.

"You can punish me when you get home," he says with a sexy grin. We hear a scream and then a wailing sound in the background. "Duty calls, I've gotta go. Love you, princess."

She smiles at the phone as she hangs up and says to me, "See? Chaos."

"I love that he still calls you princess," I say, practically swooning. But then I hear someone say my name. I look in their direction as a camera flashes in my face.

"Would you like to make a statement regarding the Brothel Debacle?" a reporter says, sticking a mic in my face.

Oh, gosh, they now have a catchy name for it.

"Yeah," I say, not caring anymore, "here's my statement." I salute him with my middle fingers, which he takes a photo of before he's escorted out by security.

The manager comes over to our table and begins to apologize to me. But he stops mid-sentence upon noticing Jadyn and looks completely horrified. "*Mrs. Mackenzie*, I didn't know you would be dining with us this evening." He looks at her like she's the celebrity.

"I didn't know I would be either, Lawrence, but Jennifer and I are old friends, and I called her on a whim after our meeting today."

"Is the Royal suite suitable? Is the staff taking good care of you?"

"The suite is what I envisioned, based on the photos." Jadyn gives him the kind of smile that seems to put him more at ease. "And I'd like to compliment you. I've had the pleasure of chatting with a lot of your staff, and many of them have been here for years. That tells me you make it a great place to work."

"I didn't feel comfortable about asking this in the meeting," he confides, "but is the hotel really getting torn down?"

"That's the plan. It's too bad really. It's a wonderful old place with a lot of character. Hopefully, I can design a new building that will honor its history."

"Thank you, ma'am. I appreciate that, but it makes my heart hurt." He shakes Jadyn's hand, departing as our waiter arrives with our food.

We've only taken a few bites when a distinguished-looking gentleman appears. He looks familiar, but I can't seem to place him.

"I see you turned down my dinner offer for a much more beautiful companion," the man says to Jadyn.

"Jennifer, I'd like you to meet Tripp Archibald," she says, introducing us and causing me to suddenly realize *who* he is.

His family, based in Kansas City, made millions in the finance industry, which Harold "Tripp" Archibald III parlayed into billions in, well, *every* industry.

"I understand you are staying at my hotel," he says to me. "I'm sorry about what's been going on in the press. I'm curious though. What made you come here?"

"Jadyn said she was staying here," I answer honestly.

"And would you have chosen this hotel otherwise?" he inquires.

Nothing like being put on the spot. "Um, it's a lovely old hotel," I reply diplomatically.

"Exactly," he says, turning toward Jadyn. "Jennifer is the client I want to come here—to seek refuge from the press, to relax in privacy, to be treated like royalty. The way it used to be."

"I got taken up in a dingy service elevator," I blurt out, causing Tripp's eyes to bulge. "But it's okay. The valet was wonderful. When I got here, I looked pretty bad. I had on slippers. It's been a rough week."

"I understand that, and I appreciate him taking care of you. What I don't appreciate is that he was forced to take you in a service elevator for privacy. We have to change that."

"If I do this project," Jadyn says, "and I'm still not sure I'm the right person for the job, it's going to be ridiculously expensive. The staff has already started sending me their wish lists, and I'm going to need to hire a lot of expert consultants—from wedding and event planners to celebrity assistants and studio heads."

"And that's exactly why you are right for the job." The man gives Jadyn a beaming smile. "I'll let you enjoy your dinner, ladies. Have a wonderful evening."

"Holy crap," I say. "I can't believe I just met *the* Tripp Archibald. I hear he's quite the ladies' man. I think he has a crush on you."

"He has a crush on my company's designs, ethics, and profitability. I know his reputation, but when it comes to work, he's all business. He and Phillip have become friends, sort of. Actually, he is trying to acquire Phillip's company."

"That's amazing."

"Except that Phillip doesn't want to sell—at least, not under the terms that have been proposed."

A sommelier comes back, bearing a bottle of wine. "Compliments of Mr. Archibald. And I might add, one of the best wines in our cellar. You must be very special guests."

"I'm here with a big shot," I tease.

She rolls her eyes. "I'm not going to talk work. And you need to eat."

WE EAT DINNER in a comfortable silence, savoring the incredible wine and delicious food. By the time we've had dessert and finished our wine, I'm raring to go.

"You're in the Royal suite. We should have a par-tay!" I say.

"Who do you want to invite to this party?"

I suspect she hasn't drunk nearly as much of the wine as I have.

I slump back in my seat when I realize I can't think of anyone.

"I think you should skip partying and get a good night's sleep. You've had just the right amount of wine to have you sleeping like a baby."

"You planned this?"

She smirks. "Maybe a little. You look like you haven't really slept in days. It's like giving a baby some Benadryl before a long drive—something that has to be timed perfectly."

"Let's go upstairs then." I give in, suddenly feeling the weight of the last few days.

When we're in the elevator, I say, "When you tear down this hotel, can you leave the bar? It was cozy. I loved it."

Although I'm pretty sure it was because of the company, not just the decor.

OCTOBER 26TH

Jennifer

"HOW DID YOUR meeting go?" I ask Jadyn as we take our seats in the plane and prepare for takeoff.

"It was good," she replies. "I don't want to be rude, but would you mind if I worked on the way home? My mind is spinning with ideas, and I'd love to get them down on paper."

"Of course not. I'll probably sleep the whole way. I'm still tired." And possibly slightly hungover.

"You've been through a lot, Jennifer," she says with a smile. "Sleep will do you good."

When we reach cruising altitude, she unfolds a large design table out of the wall, and I watch her sketch out a grand gathering space before I fall asleep.

WE LAND AT an executive airport in Kansas City, transfer to an SUV in the parking lot, and get buckled in.

She glances over at me, looking a little nervous. "Is Cade Crawford still your agent?"

"Yeah, why?"

"I didn't know if you would have heard anything through him. His brother, Carter, is Danny's agent. Since you mentioned Danny's wife when I texted you—"

"Is she going to hate me? Is she going to be mad that you

invited me?" I have a moment of panic. "Ohmigosh, does she *know* about me and Danny?"

"To my knowledge, Danny never told her about you. Or that he stopped talking to you and why. You would think something like that would make a woman feel good about her marriage."

"But not her?"

"No."

"So, do we have a story? Like, how do you and I know each other if I'm not supposed to know Danny?"

"We're old friends," Jadyn says simply.

"But isn't she going to want to know how we met?"

"If she does, I'll tell her the truth. That we met at a Nebraska game a long time ago. When I was in California for my meeting, we got back in touch."

"Okay. Why do I feel like there's something you're not telling me? Even if it's bad, tell me. I'd rather know now."

"Danny and Lori are getting a divorce. They've managed to keep it out of the press. Their attorneys won't officially file until they've signed the financial and custodial agreements, which takes place next week. I think Danny should be the one to tell you the rest though. It's not really my place."

"Are you freaking kidding me?" I yell out. My heart soars as a grin spreads across my face.

"You should see your smile." Jadyn laughs.

"I'm sorry. I know it's horrible of me, but it makes me happy. What happened?"

"While I'm really not all that surprised about them getting a divorce, I just never in a million years imagined that she would be the one to want it. She enjoys spending his money way too much."

"*She* wanted a divorce?" My hand flies up to my chest. "What's wrong with her? Danny's freaking perfection!" I narrow my eyes at her, realizing for the first time that the Danny Diamond I fell for years ago might be very different now. "Wait, did Danny turn into a jerk? Was he cheating on her? Does he have an addiction to women? Or drugs? Or alcohol?"

"Danny is and has always been a good man. He's never cheated, and he has no addictions—other than maybe working out. The rest of it, you need to hear from him. Mostly because we have differing opinions about it."

"But you and Danny are still best friends?"

"Of course we are. And we still live next door to each other. Something Lori hates. Thank goodness he never gave in on moving away. Speaking of which," she says, making a turn, "this is our neighborhood. Our houses are on a lake, which is really fun. When you look out back, you sort of feel like you're on vacation."

I take in the large homes. The bicycles in the front yards. Women pushing strollers down the sidewalks. I notice Jadyn waves at everyone we pass. The neighborhood is pretty with lots of trees, lush green lawns, and streets that seem to wind endlessly.

After numerous turns, she pulls into the driveway of a sprawling home with a beautiful, welcoming front porch that's all decked out for Halloween. I glance at the houses on each side, wondering which one is Danny's. Wondering if he's home. Or if I might catch a glimpse of him.

Jadyn hits the remote, causing the garage door to open. Just as we're pulling in, a woman comes out of the house next door. I will admit that I might have checked out Danny's wife online. It's been a long time since I've seen a photo of her, so I'm not sure if this is her or not, and it causes my mind to fill with another million questions.

Are they still living together until the divorce is final? is the first that comes to mind.

Jadyn stops, rolls down her window, and says, "Hey, Kyla. How's your little one feeling?"

Kyla smiles and tells her it wasn't an ear infection, just teething, and then we pull into the garage, and she shuts the door behind us.

We're stepping into a large laundry/mudroom when Jadyn's phone beeps.

"Shoot. I have to go pick up my younger kids from school. Phillip's meeting is running late. Do you want to come with me?" She pauses just long enough to set her bags down. "On second thought, stay here, and make yourself at home. Enjoy the peace while you can."

She leads me into an expansive kitchen with gray cabinetry, brass pulls, stainless appliances, and gleaming white marble countertops. She points to the other side of the room where next to a long dining table are more cabinets featuring a buffet and two under-counter beverage refrigerators filled with an assortment of drinks.

"Help yourself to a drink and a snack. I'll be ten minutes, tops."

She glances at the time again and then rushes out of the house.

I stand in the kitchen and look around. Their house is … different. A lot different than the tract home I grew up in and a lot different from the modern Malibu beach house I've been living in. This house is, in one word, comfortable. But it's also quite beautiful. Like something you'd see in a magazine from a design standpoint but still casual. On the buffet, there is a pedestal filled with cupcakes, covered with a domed glass. Two apothecary jars flank it, one loaded with pretzels and the other with a homemade snack mix. A wire bowl is filled with apples.

But it's the table that catches my eye. It's modern in style, yet the wood is worn and its surface marred. Probably all scratched up from having four kids, but as I glide my hand across it, I realize they aren't scratches. Numerous names are carved into the table. Part of me wonders why someone would purposefully do this to their table, but as I read all the names, I'm overcome with emotion. These are all their friends. Hundreds of them. The kind of friends who get together once a month. Whose kids are friends. People who care about each other. I don't have many people like that in my life. Over the years, a combination of Troy's drinking and his quest for fame and fortune has gotten in the way. If I had a table like this, there would only be a handful of names on it. I've missed out on so many friendships.

I walk toward the windows and take in the view of the lake. There's a library off to the left. While most of the home features a wide-open floor plan, this bookcase-filled room is sectioned off and cozy. I take a seat in a comfy chair, curl my legs up, and stare out at the lake.

I'm completely lost in thought when the front door opens. I have a moment of panic as I hear heavy footsteps instead of the sound of children coming home from school. *Did someone just break in?* My eyes sweep the area, looking for a weapon and settling on a heavy amethyst bookend.

With the bookend in my palm, I tiptoe toward the kitchen. A shirtless man is standing in front of the refrigerator, drinking milk straight out of the jug. Sweat shimmers across his muscular back. *Is he some crack addict who breaks into houses and steals milk? No, a crack addict wouldn't be built like that. Clearly, milk does a body good.*

"What do you think you're doing?" I yell out.

The guy turns at the sound of my voice. When he sees me, his eyes bug out, and he drops the milk.

Oh. My. God. It's him. Danny Diamond in the flesh.

And holy mother-effing hell.

The glass bottle bounces off the floor without breaking, but milk splashes everywhere.

I rush toward him to help clean it up.

But Danny doesn't move. He's frozen, rooted in his spot, milk on the floor and splattered on the cabinets all around him. He's drinking in the sight of me, like he was drinking the milk earlier, with force. His eyes feel like a rough caress. I look down at the workout clothes I'm wearing, wanting only comfortable traveling garments in my hungover state this morning. I remember washing my face and dabbing on some concealer and mascara. I thought I would get here, freshen up, and change before he ever saw me. This is not how I wanted to look when I met Danny Diamond again. Especially since he's still staring at me.

I find my voice. "Hey."

After all the clever and witty things I'd planned to say if I ever saw him again, all I could manage to blurt out was, *Hey.*

Great first impression, Jenn.

"Hey is for horses," Danny says back, laughing.

Has he gone mad? Did the divorce push him over the edge?

I give him a once-over. He looks a little older, a few soft crinkles around his eyes, but that is the only soft thing I can observe. Everything else is toned, hardened muscle. I remember when we stripped down to our underwear and ran into the ocean in the moonlight. He was just a rookie quarterback then. A hotshot. Still boyish. Not yet the man standing in front of me. The same muscles are there, the same level of fitness, but he looks fuller, more solid. Or maybe it's because I'm at a point in my life where I feel so weak.

We simultaneously move toward each other, drawn together, until we're mere inches apart. Both of us basking in the fact that we are in the same room after all these years. Danny's eyes move to my mouth, and in that moment, I think he might kiss me.

The front door bursts open, and children come bounding in. Backpacks hit the floor. The air fills with laughter. A teen girl and two boys stop in their tracks upon seeing us.

"You'd better clean that up before Mom gets home," the tallest boy, who I recognize as Chase, states.

"I'd let Angel lick it all up!" the other boy says.

Danny's gaze breaks, leaving me feeling cold. "That's a darn good idea, Damon," he says, moving to rustle his son's hair. "Chase, go get her. She is probably asleep in your mom's room and didn't hear us come in."

"Who are you?" the girl asks me.

It doesn't take much to know that this is Danny's daughter. They share the same brilliant blue eyes and dirty-blonde hair.

"I, uh—" I stutter because all that comes to mind is, *I'm the woman who wants to take your father in the nearest bedroom and—*

"This is Jennifer Edwards," Danny says to her.

"Like the movie star?" she asks.

"She *is* the movie star," Danny replies.

The girl scrutinizes me.

"I don't have any makeup on," I say in my defense.

"Where's Auntie Jay?" she asks, seemingly not convinced of who I am.

"She went to pick up, um, some kids. Someone else was supposed to, but she had to at the last minute," I offer as an older yellow Labrador pads slowly into the room, wags her tail at the kids, and then eagerly licks up the milk.

Danny

I'M STANDING IN Jadyn's kitchen, three of our combined six children clamoring about with the dog licking milk off my shoes, and staring at the woman who was probably the love of my life.

This isn't exactly how I expected things to go down if I were ever lucky enough to see her again.

"Why don't you guys grab some cookies, go downstairs, and work on your homework before we have to leave for the game?" I suggest to the kids.

"I can't eat cookies, Dad," Devaney says. "I'm in high school. I have to look hot."

"You're fourteen. You shouldn't worry about that."

"Whatever," she says, grabbing an apple from the island and going downstairs to the ultimate kid zone. A place to play, relax, and study. I'm redoing my house so that it's more kid-friendly, hoping to wipe the memories of being forced to behave like little adults by my soon-to-be ex from the kids' minds.

"There are wipes under the sink you can use," Damon says as he grabs a paper plate from the buffet and piles it high with snacks.

I can't get him to lift a finger at home, but at the Mackenzie house, kids are told how to behave if they want to hang out here. And they all follow the rules because they want to be here.

"If it's sticky, Auntie Jay will not be happy."

I slip off my shoes and gesture to Jennifer that I'll be right back. I step over the sticky mess, pick up the dog, and carry her downstairs, knowing, in her advanced age, she doesn't like to be separated from Chase.

As I make my way back up the stairs, I wonder if I'm dreaming. If I'll get back to the kitchen and realize that seeing Jennifer was some exercise-induced hallucination.

How could she possibly be here? Why is she here?

It's been years. I know, not long after I cut off communication with her, she started dating a drummer. I know they've never had children even though the tabloids always proclaimed she had a baby bump. I've seen photos of her on magazine covers, seen every movie she ever made, and dreamed of her many times over the years.

But I never imagined she'd be here.

"Why are you here?" I blurt out the second I get to the top of the stairs.

But she's gone.

Am I losing it? Was the milk bad?

"Because Jadyn invited me," a voice says from behind the island.

I take a few steps forward and see her down on her knees, antibacterial wipes in hand, cleaning up the floor.

"You didn't have to do that." I pull a wipe out of the plastic container. "I was coming back to clean it. I'm sorry. I was surprised to see you here. Speaking of that, why *are* you here?"

"You might be the only person in the world who doesn't know." She scrubs the floor with more vigor.

"Know what?"

"About Troy." When she looks up at me, her eyes fill with tears.

"Is he dead?" I ask, assuming the worst as I drop onto my knees next to her.

"What? No? He, um—there are photos. He and some girls. In bed. A wild night after a gig in Amsterdam. The paparazzi have been relentless. They all want a statement from me. What do they think I'm going to say? *My boyfriend cheated on me, and it hurts like hell. Yes, I was shocked. No, I had no idea.*"

"My wife had an affair for a year," I quickly confess. "I had no idea. She told me right before we were supposed to leave on a trip to celebrate our fifteenth anniversary. I realized later the reason she waited until then was because it meant she would get more, according to the prenup."

"Were you happy?"

"I thought we were."

"Did you ever think about me?" she asks as our gazes lock.

"Yes, often."

"I was there when you won your first Super Bowl. I had a pass to go out on the field. My first reaction was to run down there to congratulate you, but your wife was there, and you were holding your little girl when you received the MVP Award. I understood the joy on your face. It wasn't just because you'd won. It was also the way your little girl held on to you. She smiled and kissed your cheek. Troy is a big fan of yours. He had no idea we'd ever met. I pretended to be sick for the next championship you won. I just couldn't bear to go. It was one thing to watch you on TV, another to be there in person. I've even been invited to the ESPYs numerous times over the years. I always turn it down."

"Why?"

"Because I knew, the next time we were together, I wouldn't be so moral."

I gulp, knowing that was the same reason I couldn't be *just* her friend. She's so beautiful—long blonde hair, big blue eyes, killer body. I take in her full, lush lips, wanting nothing more than to kiss them—screw that, I want to take her by the hair, drag her to my house, throw her on the bed, and—

The garage door bursts open. Crusher, Jadyn's youngest, comes barreling into the kitchen, closely followed by Jadyn and her other two children.

"Danny!" Jadyn says, her eyes widening with surprise when she spots me on the floor. "Um, I was going to tell you about Jennifer being here before—shit."

"Shit, shit, shit," Madden yells out.

"The kids are downstairs and have cookies," I tell her son.

"Yes," Jadyn agrees. "All of you, go down there, have a snack, and get your homework done if you want to go to the game tonight."

They grab juice boxes, snacks, and their backpacks and are off to the basement. The garage door opens again, and Phillip, who must not see me and Jennifer on the floor, grabs his wife and pulls her in for a deep kiss.

"Sorry I'm late. I promise to make it up to you later," he suggests, his hand moving to caress her backside while his lips slide down her neck. "I missed you."

I stand up and hold my hand out for Jennifer, who takes it.

"You playing hide-and-seek with the kids?" he asks when he sees me, but he stops speaking when Jennifer follows me up. "Um, Jadyn?" he says, turning toward his wife and narrowing his eyes at her but not appearing as surprised as he should be.

I want to contemplate that, but Jennifer's hand is in mine, and it makes my heart pound like I just ran fifty yards for a touchdown.

"I know. Okay," Jadyn says to Phillip. "But I had to offer. And I was shocked and *thrilled* when she took me up on it. We literally just walked in the door from the airport when I had to leave her here because *you* bailed on picking up the kids." She turns to me and Jennifer. "I'm sorry. I certainly didn't expect you to see each other after all this time when Danny is … just all sweaty."

Jennifer slides her hand out of mine, leaving it feeling empty. Lonely. Incomplete.

"I'm not that sweaty," I counter, but I know I am.

Jennifer is probably repulsed.

"I told you, playing matchmaker is like playing with matches. You'll get burned," Phillip says sternly to his wife.

"You didn't want me to come?" Jennifer asks Phillip, looking stricken.

Phillip gives her the same smile he gives Jadyn when she's pissed. The one that instantly calms her down. "My wife doesn't like to be told what to do. Yesterday, after her meeting, she was debating on all the pros and cons of inviting you. After an hour's worth of texts, I told her I thought it was a bad idea." He grins. "That pretty much guaranteed she would contact you. I'm really more surprised that you came." He walks over and gives her a hug. "Surprised but glad. It's been a long time. I'm sorry for what you're going through."

I roll my eyes. This is why Phillip, who once told Jadyn that he'd never be able to afford the kind of house I could buy, has almost surpassed me in wealth. His good looks, sincerity, and his ability to sell anything to anyone mean he's taken his dad's already successful company to new heights. Not to mention, he has his equally talented wife, who probably just signed a contract to rebuild an iconic Beverly Hills hotel today.

"I'm glad I'm here, too," Jennifer says, practically melting into Phillip's arms.

I should be the one hugging her, I think, feeling jealous.

"Why were you two on the floor?" he asks.

"I spilled milk," I say, sounding dumb, like the girl in *Dirty Dancing* who says, "I carried a watermelon"—a movie line Jadyn often quotes during awkward moments.

"And I was helping to clean it up," Jennifer adds.

"Although Angel took care of most of it. My son's idea." I chuckle.

"The boy is smart," Phillip says.

"Damon can come up with a million ways to slack."

"He's a leader," Phillip counters. "Nothing wrong with knowing how to delegate. Isn't that what you do on the field? *Here, you take the ball, so I don't get hit*," he teases.

Jennifer laughs. And keeps laughing. Like she hasn't laughed in a while.

"Quarterbacks do that, don't they?" She giggles some more.

A broad smile spreads across my face.

Her laughing reminds me of how we met. I said something that made her laugh and then didn't leave her side the rest of the night. I wonder what my life would have been like if I hadn't stopped talking to her. But I know. Talking would have led to seeing, seeing would have led to touching, touching would have led to sex. There is no doubt in my mind that the sex would have been monumental, intense. Probably better than winning the big game.

Just simply helping her up brought a rush of the kind of passion that I hadn't felt in a really long time.

I've been blaming Lori for the failure of our marriage. She's the one who was unfaithful. She's the one who ended it. *But would she have cheated if we had truly been happy?*

I know my feelings for her were never the same after she accused Jadyn and me of having an affair. And they took another hit when she got mad at me for staying at the hospital with Phillip when a pregnant Jadyn nearly lost her life after a car accident.

I had plenty of opportunities to cheat.

But I never did.

And it wasn't my love for Lori that stopped me. It was the love I had for my children.

"Let's go out on the deck and have a beer," Phillip says, finally releasing Jennifer.

Jennifer

DANNY PUTS HIS hand on the small of my back, causing shivers to run down my spine. Good shivers. The kind that seem to connect directly to my lady parts.

I shake my head, mentally chastising myself. *Your long-time significant other cheated on you. You need to deal with that. Lick your wounds. Pick yourself up and move on. You should not be thinking about doing it with Danny Diamond.*

But the man is like sex on a stick, waiting to be licked. If I'm being honest with myself, that's exactly why I came here. It wasn't just to get away from the paparazzi.

"Why don't you go take a quick shower?" Jadyn says to Danny.

She mentioned earlier that she didn't want me to see him again for the first time when he was hot and sweaty, but I disagree. It's exactly how I should have seen him. Because I've been seeing a version of him this way in my dreams for years.

We were at a party. Got introduced. He shook my hand as his blue eyes drank me in. It was intimate. Perfect. I was being my loud, crazy self, but in that moment, it felt like time slowed. I was dating my hot costar at the time, but there had never been any talk of exclusivity. I'd been drinking a little. Danny made me feel insanely hot, and I couldn't help it. I wanted him. So, I grabbed a bottle of champagne from the party and told him we were going somewhere quiet to talk. Although talking was the last thing I wanted to do with Danny Diamond. I wanted him to throw me into the sand and screw my brains out. I even made the first move and kissed him.

But then he told me he was married.

After *that kiss*, there was no way I was going to let him leave. I would take whatever time I could get with him. We sat in the sand and talked for hours, each of us spilling all our secrets to the other. All the things we feared about how our lives would end up. Danny told me about his wife and her jealousy. He beamed when he showed me pictures of their baby girl. He was concerned he would end up hating his wife, and their relationship would go down in flames.

He told me he'd never met someone like me. Never felt things so fast. I told him I could never be with a married man. He told me he would never cheat.

Then we just sat there, staring into each other's eyes, wondering what could have been had we met earlier in life. I'd had enough to drink that I blurted out exactly what I was thinking.

We talked about true love. Soul mates. And we both knew, without a doubt, that's what we were. He caressed my cheek as we spoke. I held his other hand and kept pressing my lips into it.

Phillip thrusts a beer toward me, bringing me back to the present. I take a long sip. Because of Troy's struggle with addiction, I didn't keep beer in the house and avoided alcohol out of respect for him. *How long has it been since I've had a crisp, cold beer?* And it tastes even better with the cool breeze coming off the lake and the sun's rays warming the top of my head.

"This tastes so good," I mutter.

"The first rule here is, you don't drink until we toast," Phillip says.

I put my head down, embarrassed. "Jadyn mentioned that. Sorry, I forgot."

"It's okay," Jadyn says. "We just try to appreciate moments like these."

Phillip smiles at his wife and squeezes her hand. "And we have a lot to toast to tonight."

They raise their bottles in the air, so I follow suit.

"To a few brief moments of quiet before all hell breaks loose downstairs," Phillip says.

"And to a gorgeous evening," Jadyn adds.

"And to Jennifer coming back into our lives," Danny says, his gaze settled on me as we clink our bottles. I take a drink—once again prematurely because he turns and presses his bottle against Jadyn's. "And to the woman who got her here."

I'm touched. By all of it. Their friendship. Their family. Their inviting me into their home. Who does that?

Before I moved to California, I had lots of friends. But I left home, and they stayed, and then we lost touch. Not the case with Danny, Phillip, and Jadyn. Their friendships have only deepened over time. It makes me long to be a part of it.

Although he didn't talk much more about his wife that night, he did mention she was jealous of his best friend. When I went to the Nebraska game, I understood why. Jadyn and Danny's closeness was unnerving. Men and women couldn't be just friends.

I thought there must be something going on. But then I saw her and Phillip together and knew she wasn't a threat.

It's apparent that they've been his rock through the divorce.

The moment of silence passes quickly, and before I have swallowed my third sip of beer, kids run out of a door under the deck and into the backyard, the two older boys wrestling each other and possibly in a fight. As they roll across the ground, I see the smiles on their faces. Damon gets pinned by Chase and taps out. Best friends, too. No matter what. I can just tell.

Chase gets up, wipes the grass from his pants, helps Damon up, and then takes a phone out of his back pocket, saying, "I win."

We watch as he types something into his phone.

Jadyn's phone immediately buzzes.

She scans the message and then stands up. "Chase Mackenzie, I'm going to take your phone away. You know the rules."

His eyes get big, and he looks sincere when he says, "I didn't see you up there!" He gives her a grin. "I know you had a busy trip, Mom. You shouldn't have to cook. Sound like a plan?"

Jadyn smiles at her son. "You're very thoughtful, Chase. Yes, if you'll go make sandwiches for everyone now and be dressed and ready to leave for your football game in an hour, we'll all go out for pizza after."

Chase and Damon cheer and wrangle all the kids back inside.

But then Jadyn looks at me. "Oh, shoot, um, maybe you going out isn't a good idea. Although I doubt anyone would realize who you were if you wore a ball cap. I'd leave you home with Danny, but he and Phillip help coach the team."

"I love pizza," I say, not wanting to be left out. "And football."

"I should probably go shower," Danny says.

I'm hoping he'll ask me to join him, but know that probably wouldn't be appropriate.

"I could use a shower, too," I practically whimper.

Jadyn presses her lips together, trying not to smile, and I realize how that just sounded.

"I, uh, didn't mean, like, *with* him," I lie. But then I glance at Danny, who looks slightly crushed, so I start babbling, "I mean, I'd love to shower with you sometime, Danny. Uh, I mean, I just—the traveling. I don't know what I'm even saying. I'm sorry. Just stop me."

"Why don't I show you up to the guest room before I leave?" Danny offers, his eyes soft with understanding. "You can freshen up, and I'll meet you all back here in a few."

I drain the rest of my beer, feeling tipsy the second we're in the house. Or maybe I feel tipsy because Danny is holding my hand as he leads me back to the garage, out a side door, and then up a set of stairs I didn't notice before.

"Jadyn recently turned the attic into a combination office slash guest room. The good news is, it's quiet up here."

The space is gorgeous. The ceiling follows the roofline and features wood beams wrapped with metal. The walls shimmer in a warm pink. The girlie color is offset by numerous architectural drawings set in black metal frames. A dark wood drafting table is set against a wall with an inspiration design board hanging above it. On the opposite wall two antique barn doors are slid open, one side filled with binders full of swatches and the other side featuring a kitchenette with a glimmering pink and gold glass backsplash. This area also has a round table across from a seating area filled with what looks to be the most comfortable couches in the history of mankind.

My head is on a swivel as I try to take it all in, but Danny leads me through the space without a word. He slides open a barn door at the end of the room to reveal an adorable bedroom suite, one that looks straight out of an HGTV episode. One wall is covered in reclaimed wood. A cream linen padded bed sits in front of it, draped in fluffy white bedding. A soft, pastel wool rug covers the wood floors, and modern gold metal chairs are dressed with white fur. A crystal chandelier dangles from the ceiling.

"It's so pretty. I might never leave," I blurt out.

Danny lets go of my hand and turns toward me.

And I suddenly feel like just a girl. Standing in front of a boy. And nothing else matters. Not where we've been or what we've been through to get to this exact spot. Just like we stood on the beach that night. When it was almost dawn.

"I can't believe you're here," he says.

"I can't either," I reply, our eyes locked.

We don't speak. We don't have to. Just the fact that we are here says volumes about what could be.

But then he goes, "Why are you really here?" His tone is brusque, almost irritated. "You just need a place to hide out from the press?"

"I, uh …" I say, getting distracted by his chest, noticing a salty residue clinging to his collarbone. *Is it gross that I want to run my finger through it and taste it?*

"You, *uh*, what?" he asks, causing me to catch the squint of his eye. The hurt behind those gorgeous baby blues.

"That's not an easy question to answer. We haven't really caught up yet."

"I'm getting a divorce, and you're going through a rough spell," he says.

Now, I see why he looks all bunched up. He really thinks I only came to hide out.

"I left him," I say, causing the tension in his jaw to soften ever so slightly.

"And Jadyn invited you."

"Yes," I say, feeling ready to cry. "I was afraid to come, but being able to see you again … I just couldn't pass it up. And it makes no sense really. I look horrible. I haven't slept much lately. And I thought you were still married. But I had to come."

He studies me. There is a large mirror decorating the bedroom, and I suddenly see myself reflected in it. My eyes are just visible over Danny's shoulder. I see the fear in them. The sadness. For what I know I lost.

And I'm not talking about my relationship with Troy.

"Why?" he says again.

He is just like me, I realize. Broken. Hurt.

"Because I've never stopped thinking about you. When you cut off contact, it broke my heart." He looks like he's going to say something, but I keep going, "No, that's not right. When we stopped talking, it was like you took a piece of my heart. Or I left it with you. I'm not sure." As I speak, I feel bolder, more sure of myself. "I was in love with you, Danny. I had never in my life felt what I felt when I was with you. Considering that nothing really happened between us, you obviously made an impact on me."

He doesn't reply. Doesn't tell me he felt the same way. Instead, he nods and then walks past me and into the bathroom where he turns on the shower.

"It's got a tankless heater, so you won't run out of hot water, just takes a while to get all the way up here."

"Thanks," I say, following him into the bathroom, which, although spacious, feels small, Danny's big body filling up the area.

He tries to slide past me, but his naked chest grazes across the front of my shirt. I swallow hard. He keeps moving toward the door, like he can't get away from me fast enough.

"I'm sorry I made you spill the milk," I say for lack of anything better.

"It's okay," he says softly, stopping. He's close to me, and he definitely doesn't stink. Instead, he smells like he did that night at the beach. The salt mixed with his manly scent. "I have to be honest with you, Jennifer. I've been through a lot over the last few months. I don't know if I could handle you coming back in my life, only to be split apart again. In other words, don't start something with me you don't fully intend to finish."

He walks out the door, leaving me feeling completely confused.

I'm not sure what to do. I don't really need a shower. I took one just this morning. I meant it as a joke. Sorta.

But I strip off my clothes anyway, lost in thought, the emotion behind what Danny said hitting me full force. He's afraid I'll go back to Troy. That we'll—

"Oh!" I hear and then see Danny standing at the doorway, his eyes wide. "Um, sorry. Didn't know you'd be naked already." He smiles and shakes his head. "I came back to tell you I'm sorry for acting like a jerk." He pulls me in tightly, the skin on our chests touching and filling me with desire. "I'm glad you're here, Jennifer."

I'm ready for him to kiss me. To strip off his shorts and take me in the shower.

Instead, he walks back out the door.

Danny

I LEAVE QUICKLY, the thought of Jennifer's naked body on my mind as I race down the stairs and through the front yard to the safety of my house, hoping none of the neighbors notice me leaving Phillip and Jadyn's house with a raging boner. One touch, and I feel like a teenager again. Heck, that's not true. More like a middle schooler. I could control it better than this in high school.

It's been over five months since I've had sex. Five months since my wife left. My kids have held my focus. They were devastated. They had a million questions. They blamed me. They blamed her. In the end, they wanted to stay here, in their house. They quickly realized their mother was off with someone new and didn't want to spend time with them. Not that she really ever did before. To her, our kids were just another status symbol. She hired nannies because she couldn't handle the messy parts of childrearing. She had a housekeeper and a cook for the rest. Part of me wondered what the hell she did all day. Screwed around, obviously.

But even thoughts of Lori's betrayal can't quell my arousal.

As I step into a cold shower, my thoughts turn back to Jennifer Edwards. Who is clearly in distress. Who would totally sleep with me on the rebound.

And then go back to Hollywood where she came from.

It's the other reason I haven't been with anyone. I can't bring someone into my children's lives, only to have them leave.

Those thoughts quickly fade as I picture Jennifer standing there, naked. I soap up my hand and go at it. I'm almost there when there's a knock on my door and a wail.

"Dad!"

I jump out of the shower, thinking someone is bleeding, my manhood responding by shrinking to its normal state. I wrap a towel around my waist and fling open the door.

Devaney is standing in my room, crocodile tears rolling out of her eyes, clearly upset.

"What's wrong?"

"Mom canceled on our spa day for Saturday. She and *Richard* are going out of town. Dad, she promised. It's homecoming. We planned it for months! I'm supposed to get my hair highlighted, my makeup done, and everything!"

I hug my daughter, feeling disgusted with my wife. *How could she do this again? Put some guy in front of her kids?*

"She'll make it up to you," I lie.

"No, she won't, Dad."

She escapes my hug and plops dramatically on the bed. "Chase said he'd take me anywhere I wanted to go and that we'd have more fun than a stupid day at the spa."

"What do you think would be more fun?"

She sighs as tears trickle down her face.

Lori has caused her so many tears. That's the real reason I fought so hard during this divorce. Sole custody. The money I don't even care about. But the kids are like pawns to Lori. Small pieces of her life, just like the football wives club and her charities. Having children made her appear nurturing and soft as opposed to the conniving bitch that she really was. For a while, she pretended to want them and fought me for joint custody but, once I sweetened the pot with more money than required in the prenuptial agreement, she backed off. Just last week, we verbally finalized our divorce agreement. Once we sign it next week, we will file, it will be presented to a judge, and in thirty days, it will be over.

I want her out of my life, but I know, because of the kids, she never will be.

There were only two things she didn't ask for. The house and my Ferrari, which, fortunately for me, are two things she's always hated.

"I want to go to Paris instead of homecoming," Devaney says, pulling me back to the situation at hand.

"Paris, France?" I ask.

"Yes."

"I'm afraid I can't swing that, Dani. I have a game on Monday night. What do you want to do in Paris?"

"I don't know." She shrugs. "Things."

"Is there somewhere closer you might want to go?" I ask gently. "And do you really want to miss your first homecoming dance? Won't your friends be disappointed? I thought you were all going together."

"My friends have been sort of mad at me since I made varsity cheerleading. They say I'm too good for them now. If it wasn't for cheerleading, I would hate school. I miss Chase."

"He'll be there next year."

She brightens slightly. "He said he'd be my date."

"Do you want that?"

She sighs. "Dad, you know I love Chase, but I can't take an eighth grader to a high school dance. It would ruin me."

"Sounds like you need some new friends."

"Exactly," she says. "Mine need to grow up. But the problem is, Dad, you don't want me to. Tomorrow night, there is a slumber party at the head cheerleader's house after the game. All the cheerleaders are going but me."

"That's because she's a senior."

She throws her hands up in the air. "I need to just quit then. My friends are mad at me because I made varsity, so they won't be friends with me. You won't let me make new friends because they are older than me, and you worry that I'm going to get in trouble like you used to."

"What makes you think—"

"I've heard enough of the stories to know that, back then, you weren't like you are now."

"How am I now?"

"No fun."

Her words cut me to the core. I slowly lower myself to the bed to sit, halfway afraid I'll fall down if I don't. *When did I become no fun?*

"You're way too strict. You don't trust me anymore. It's like you've turned into Mom."

I take a deep breath. "I do trust you, Devaney."

"But you don't trust other people," she says, finishing my sentence. "Just because you were a troublemaker doesn't mean I'm going to be. I promise, I won't do anything to embarrass you."

"I would never be embarrassed of you. You're my pride and joy. I just worry, sweetheart."

"I know you do, but you have to let me grow up. I promise, I'll try to do it slowly."

I can't help but smile. She's been telling me that since she was in kindergarten.

"So, this party, you'll be staying there all night. No going out?"

She nods.

"Okay, you can go. But I expect you to be responsible. To call me if anything goes on that makes you uncomfortable. All you have to do—"

"I know, Dad. I can pretend to be sick, and you'll come and get me, no questions asked."

"And what about Saturday? Maybe Jadyn can take you."

"Maybe. That, or I'll just hang out with Chase. Thanks, Dad," she says, practically skipping out of the room. She stops in the doorway and turns around. "Dad, how does Auntie Jay know Jennifer Edwards?"

"Uh, they met a long time ago, just after you were born, at a Nebraska football game."

"How come I've never gotten to meet her? That was forever ago."

"They just recently got back in touch, I think."

"Because of what Troy did to her?" she asks.

"Yeah, I think so."

"I read online that she's been taking it hard. I can't imagine how awful that must be for her. To see pictures like that of someone you love with someone else. Did Mom cheat on you with Richard before she left us?"

"Why do you ask that?"

"Because there is a photo in their house where they are together, kissing. She had the red highlights, and she got them changed to blonde before she moved out."

My daughter is too smart for her own good sometimes.

"Did you ask your mother about that?"

"No."

"Why not?"

"Because I don't think she'd tell me the truth." She gives me her puppy-dog eyes. "But I know you would."

"Honey, marriage is hard. It takes two to make a marriage work and two to make it fail."

"I already know she did. I overheard Auntie Jay talking about it. I know I shouldn't have been listening, but I did. Did you ever cheat on Mom?"

"No. Never," I emphatically tell her.

"Did you ever want to?"

Only once, I think.

She continues, "I thought you met your true love, got married, and lived happily ever after."

She considers this for a moment while I try to think of something comforting to tell her. I can't tell her that her mother wasn't my true love. That I met my true love after I got married. After she was already born.

"Mom says you just fell out of love."

I nod. I don't trust myself to say anything else.

"Then maybe she wasn't really your true love."

"I've told you and your brother this many times. Make good choices because the consequences of your actions can affect the rest of your life. It's something my dad told me when I got married, and I've lived by that. I always think ahead. So, while there were other pretty women in the world, I knew ahead of time what the consequences would be if I did cheat. That it would destroy my marriage, possibly cause you kids hurt. For me, that wasn't worth it."

"So, you stayed together because of me and Damon?"

"I loved your mother, Devaney."

"Do you think you will ever fall in love again? Maybe she's still out there, you know, waiting for you."

"Who?" I ask, not following.

"Your true love."

"How would you feel about that?" I can't help but ask. "If I met someone. Fell in love."

"Dad," she says, giving me an exaggerated eye roll, "you're supposed to love with your heart, not your head."

"Who told you that?" It sure as hell wasn't me. I want her thinking with her head, not her body.

"Chase."

"Chase is a smart young man, but that's not exactly true. You fall in love with your heart, but sometimes, especially when you're young and hormones are running wild, you can feel like you're in love when really—"

"Dad, this isn't about me and Chase possibly having sex someday."

My eyes get huge.

"Have you thought about having sex with Chase? Does he want to, like now? Do you like him?"

"He's my best friend; of course I like him."

"You kissed him when you were younger."

"And I've kissed him since then. And I'll probably kiss him again," she states.

"You have? You will?" *What the f—?*

"Sure, it's no big deal," she says. "He's sweet to me. Sometimes, when I'm sad, I sneak over to his house. Sometimes, I even sleep with him."

I don't care if he is Phillip's son; I'm going to kill him. Now.

She gives me a dramatic eye roll as I ball up my fists in anger. "It's not like that, Dad. He's not my boyfriend. We aren't going out or anything. He just … well, he makes me feel safe. Like everything will be okay. Like how he told me he'd take me anywhere I wanted to go. He is the one who said he'd take me on their plane to Chicago or New York or Paris."

"Devaney, no matter what's going on in our lives, you can come to me about anything. I'm always here for you, and I won't judge or freak out. I promise."

"Dad"—she laughs—"you just about had a stroke when I told you I slept with Chase."

I laugh along with her. "You're right. I just about did."

"It's okay. You survived me getting my period, and you didn't freak out too bad. You're a good dad. I don't tell you very often, but you are."

"Thanks." I kiss the top of her head. "I love you."

"I love you, too. You'd better hurry. We have to leave in, like, five minutes for the game." As I run into my closet to grab clothes, she yells out, "Wear something cool. Jennifer freaking Edwards is going with us. She's pretty. She's single. Maybe you should try to impress her."

I'm ready to reply with all the reasons I shouldn't, but when I stick my head out of the closet, she's gone.

NOW, I'M STANDING on the sideline, getting ready for the eighth grade game to start, and I am scanning the crowd, looking for Jennifer, when I notice Devaney sitting next to Chase. He's dressed in his full uniform and pads, and he should be out, warming up with the team. Instead, his arm is across the back of the bleacher, and she's leaning against it. His full attention is on her, and I can tell she's confiding in him about something. It suddenly hits me. Their friendship is like Phillip and Jadyn's. They've been best friends their whole lives.

I lean over toward Phillip, who is standing on the sideline next to me. "Did you know my daughter has been sneaking over to your house and sleeping with your son?"

Phillip's expression doesn't show surprise. And he has never been a good liar. He doesn't look me in the eyes, just kicks the dirt. "She's been upset about the divorce. Nothing is going on."

"But it could. They're teenagers now."

"Jadyn slept with me every night for months after her parents died when we were seniors. Nothing happened."

"That's because you were an idiot," I tease.

"Jadyn told Dani to tell you the truth."

"She sort of did tonight, but what I don't understand is why neither of you told me."

"It's important your children know they can trust you. Yes, you have to be a disciplinarian, but parenting is so much more than that. Did you lie to your parents?" he asks me even though he knows the answer.

"Yeah; otherwise, I would have gotten in trouble!"

"The things you lied about, are those things you'd want your daughter to do?"

"Heck no."

"That's my point. We'd rather our kids talk to us. We talk in advance about risks and consequences *before* they do it. We decide together what's best. Dani is in high school now. Older boys, bigger parties—you want her to tell you about all those things. Not to mention, sex."

"That's what her mother is for," I scoff.

"Do you and Lori share the same feelings regarding sex? Do you really want her taking advice from someone with your wife's morals?"

"Probably not," I admit.

"Plus, Jadyn says that divorce is hard on kids, especially girls. They dream of fairy-tale love. They see their parents having that, and then the idea gets shattered."

"And how do I combat it? I'm not getting back together with Lori."

"I would hope not. Just be open with Dani. Talk to her. Chase is the least of your worries," Phillip says.

That sets my heart beating fast again. Especially when Chase heads out on the field, and I watch Dani wander by herself to the concession stand. A group of high school boys looks at her and then smirks at each other. And I know that look. I've had that look. And I know exactly what those boys are thinking right now.

I might have to go kill them.

"Calm down," Phillip says. "Dani is a pretty girl. Boys are going to notice her. You have to teach her how to handle herself."

"Kicking a boy in the balls is one of the first things I ever taught her."

"Chase and Damon always watch out for her. Remember the black eye Chase got last semester?"

"Yeah. He said he ran into—"

"An eighth grader's fist," Phillip finishes my sentence. "He was saying stuff about Dani."

"What kind of stuff?"

"That she was a slut."

"Oh my God! Is she?" I panic that I'm a failure as a father.

"I thought your only goal for your children was to keep your son off the pipe and your daughter off the pole," Phillip teases, reminding me of what I said one night when I was drunk and Lori was pregnant with Devaney.

"I want to keep her off *everything*!" I reply, getting riled up. "Who was the little shit who said that?"

"Nathan Matthews."

"Isn't he a running back? Little guy?"

"Yeah, he couldn't take on Chase by himself, so he had a couple of friends jump him," Phillip says.

"Why?"

"Because Chase grabbed him at school one day and told him, if he said another word about Dani, he'd bust his ass."

"Does Devaney know?"

"Of course she knows," Phillip says with a laugh. "She got angry with Chase. Told him she could take care of herself. It was one of the few fights they'd ever had. Turns out, Nathan had a crush on Dani and couldn't figure out how to get her attention, so he was mean to her."

I rub my hand across my face, stressed. "I do remember teasing the girls I liked. We were kind of dumb when we were young, huh?"

Just as I say the words, Jennifer and Jadyn stroll across the field toward us.

"Try not to act that way now," Phillip teases.

"How am I supposed to act?"

"Be nice to her maybe? She looks good."

"She sure does," I say with the kind of regretful sigh that usually comes from my daughter when she's being dramatic.

"You were young back then, Danny. You did what you thought was right."

"Do you think it was the right thing?"

"I do think you made the right decision then but, now, you have the chance to follow your heart. If you're happy, Danny, your kids will be happy."

"You think so? Devaney told me I should dress nice because Jennifer was coming to the game. She's a little starstruck yet not. Also, I have no idea why Jennifer is even here. And I certainly don't want to be her rebound sex."

"You don't want to have sex with her? Wow. Lori must have really screwed you up—"

"What? Of course I want to have sex with her, but I don't want it to be *just* sex. I am a father. I can't go around having casual sex. If I do, Devaney will think it's okay for her."

"They usually go to Lori's every other weekend," Phillip suggests. "She doesn't have to know."

"It figures, the one weekend I actually have something I want to do, Lori decides to go out of town."

"You mean, *someone* you want to do?" Phillip says with a laugh.

"Shut up."

Jadyn saunters over, kisses Phillip full on the lips, and then says, "Good luck," while Jennifer stands awkwardly in front of me, which is weird.

The Jennifer I used to know was never awkward. She was crazy and bold and always laughing.

Not that I'm much better. In college, I would have strutted up to her, grabbed her, and kissed her just for the fun of it. Or had some stupid pick-up line that I could get away with because of who I was and how I looked.

Instead, I say, "Enjoy the game."

"I'm sure I will," she replies and then leans closer to me. "But I have to be honest; I'm looking forward to after the game." My heart feels like it's going to beat out of my chest. She wants me to see her naked again. "I can't tell you the last time I had pizza."

Or not.

Jennifer

"KILL ME NOW," I say to Jadyn as we take our seats in the bleachers for the start of the game.

"Why now?" she asks as she waves down at her two younger sons, who wanted to sit on the ground in front of the bleachers and play in the dirt instead of sit up by us.

"I think I just made Danny think I don't want to see him again."

"Because you said you wanted pizza?"

"When he showed me to my room—which is fantastic by the way. Seriously, when I get a new place, you have to help me decorate it, like, if you have the time. I know you're really busy," I word-vomit.

"I'd be happy to help you, but back to when he showed you to your room."

"Yes. Sorry. It's like I'm a bundle of nerves when I'm around him. It's so much pressure."

"Jennifer, it's been a long time since you've seen each other. It's going to be a little awkward."

"I know. It's just that, when I imagined seeing him again, I swore, I'd just straight-up pounce on him. Instead, there were kids and a dog and milk and me naked."

"Wait, *naked*?"

"You were saying that Danny was hot and sweaty and that wasn't how I should see him, but it's exactly how I should have seen him. Because he was shirtless and wet and all muscles, and it reminded me of the night we'd spent on the beach. On a mutual dare, we'd stripped down to our underwear and run into the water. It was freezing, and I was screaming and laughing. But the second he pulled me into his arms to warm me up, I forgot all about the cold and could only think about him. The way his strong arms felt wrapped around me, how his dark blond hair glowed in the moonlight, and the sound of his sexy laugh. It's a moment I've cherished. A moment forever etched in my mind. I guess I just didn't imagine him seeing me and being so shocked that he dropped the milk."

"Who dropped the milk?" an overdressed woman with teased auburn hair and jewels that belong at a red carpet event rather than a middle school football game says, sitting down on the other side of Jadyn.

"Uh, hey, Lori," Jadyn says.

Lori? As in Danny's wife? Of course it has to be her. Her son is playing. She's here to watch.

Not that I've been watching the game. I've been babbling in Jadyn's ear. I didn't even stop when she stood up to cheer about something.

"Danny dropped milk on my kitchen floor. The dog licked up most of it, so it wasn't a big deal," Jadyn states flatly.

I could cut the tension between them with a knife. I figure Lori will ask who I am, but she doesn't even acknowledge my presence.

"Did you hear that Richard and I will be off to Bermuda for a long weekend?" Lori asks Jadyn.

"I thought you were taking Dani to the spa on Saturday? She's been looking forward to it."

Lori waves her hand through the air, dismissing it. "I didn't cancel the appointments. *Devaney* can still go."

"By herself? It was supposed to be a special mother-daughter thing before her first homecoming dance. She's nervous about it."

"Why would she be nervous? She loves school. She's beautiful, and she made varsity cheerleading. She has nothing to worry about."

"She's nervous because she's starting over, kind of. And because Chase and Damon won't be there with her."

"I'm sure she'd rather take a friend to the spa than go with her mother anyway. And she needs some new friends. Someone a little more up to her caliber."

"I'll go with her then," Jadyn replies.

"Of course, Jadyn to the rescue." Lori rolls her eyes. "*As usual.*"

I notice Jadyn's hand curl tightly into a ball. I half-expect her to clock Lori.

"Well, thank you, I guess. Now, I don't have to feel guilty."

If I were Jadyn, I would go off on this woman.

Instead, Jadyn says, "So, Bermuda?"

"Yes, Richard is just so sweet. He totally pampers me. Unlike my soon-to-be ex-husband, who was too wrapped up in himself."

"Danny always did nice things for you. In fact, the trip he had planned for your wedding anniversary would have been amazing, not to mention the custom earrings he had made for you. I notice that you are wearing them," she says, her jaw tightly clenched.

"I earned them. You have no idea what it's like to be married to Danny Diamond."

I lean forward, blurting out, "But, hey, at least he gives good diamond."

"That's exactly what Richard said!" Lori laughs wholeheartedly and then says, "I don't think we've met." As she's laughing, her hand flies up.

Jadyn snatches it midair, holding it tight and staring at a diamond solitaire on her finger. "New ring?"

"Yes." Lori beams. "That's why we're going to Bermuda. To celebrate our engagement."

"But you're not divorced yet," Jadyn says, her anger apparent.

"It's just a formality at this point. We've agreed on almost everything. Most of it was spelled out in the prenup. Danny wants sole custody of the kids, and honestly, that's fine with me. I think it's best for them to be able to continue to live in their home and not have to traipse back and forth between his place and mine. I'll still be a big part of their lives, of course.

"But I have to tell you about the proposal. It was so romantic; I'm practically giddy. We were house-hunting. Richard does quite well, naturally, as one of the top physicians in the country, but once the divorce is final, we'll be able to afford something a little more spacious than his bachelor pad. Although I do have to say that I have so many fond memories of being together in that place; we might not be able to sell—"

Jadyn stands up in the middle of Lori's rambling and cheers,

"Go, Damon! Go!"

Damon breaks a tackle and sprints down the field and into the end zone, causing Jadyn to clap and wave her little paper pom-pom in the air.

When she sits back down, she turns to Lori. "Your son just scored a touchdown. You might wanna cheer for him. Oh my gosh, where are my manners? Lori, I'd like to introduce you to my friend, Jennifer Edwards."

Lori gives me a cursory glance. "Like the movie star?"

"Not *like* the movie star," Jadyn says brightly. "She *is* the movie star. She flew back from Los Angeles with me today. She's the reason Danny dropped the milk. He was so surprised to see her."

"Why wouldn't he be surprised?" Lori asks, looking perplexed. "He's seen all her movies. How do you two know each other?"

"You've seen all her movies because she's always been Danny's celebrity crush," Jadyn says.

And that makes me feel all warm and fuzzy inside.

Chase, who I just now realized plays both on offense and defense, intercepts a pass and sprints down the field to score again as the time runs out on the half. Jadyn does more screaming and cheering while Lori stays in her seat and glares at me.

She's a little scary to be honest. Bye-bye, warm fuzzies.

ONCE THE CROWD settles down and the team runs to the sideline, Jadyn turns to Lori and whispers, "Congratulations. I'm so happy for you and Dick Rash. See you later."

She grabs my arm, pulling me down the bleachers and toward her children.

When we're standing safely on the ground, she mutters, "Not."

"Holy smokes," I say. "What was that all about? And is she really marrying a man named Dick Rash?"

Jadyn doesn't get the chance to reply because Danny is right there.

He places his hand on the small of my back, leans in close, and says, "So, what did you think of the first half?"

"Are you touching me just because your wife is here?"

"Lori's here?" he asks, his hand moving off me so fast, you'd think he got burned.

"Wait," Phillip says, "Jennifer, did you say *marrying*?"

"Yes," Jadyn replies for me. "Lori and Richard got engaged. That's why she canceled on Dani. They are going to Bermuda to celebrate."

Her son, Ryder, jumps up to get her attention. "Mom, can we go to the concession stand now?"

"Sure, sweetie." She turns back to me and says, "We'll be right back."

Phillip follows her, giving her a smack on the butt before he veers off to go into the locker room.

"But our divorce isn't even final," Danny says incredulously.

"It wasn't when she cheated on you either, so I don't know why that would be a surprise," I blurt out.

"You're right."

I give him a conspiratorial grin and bump his side with my elbow. "And you ought to take some comfort in the fact that she's marrying a man named Dick Rash."

"You're right again," he says with a laugh. "I do. Lori always said Danny Diamond sounded like a porn star name."

"Will you strip for me sometime?" I whisper in his ear.

"Will you do *what* sometime?" his son, who I didn't even see standing here, asks.

"Uh … oh, Jennifer wanted to know if she could get her favorite kind of pizza tonight," Danny fibs.

"What is your favorite?" Damon asks me.

Based on his facial expression, I can tell he takes pizza very seriously.

Danny answers for me, "Her favorite is extra pepperoni and extra cheese on a thick crust."

"Pepperoni is my favorite, too," Damon says, leaving us to head to the locker room.

"I can't believe you remember that," I whisper.

"It's what you said you wished we could have for breakfast. I remember every single detail of that night, Jenn. You had a profound effect on me."

"But not enough for you to leave your wife."

"It killed me to say good-bye to you. I would have left Lori in a heartbeat, but I couldn't leave Devaney." His eyes get misty, and he lowers his head. "I can't talk about this here."

"Okay," I reply, my own eyes filling with tears. All this time, I thought it was me. I want to throw my arms around him, hug him with all my might, and never let him go.

"I need to get to the locker room with the team," he says, walking away from me.

Jadyn comes back from the concession stand, her younger children happily stuffing their mouths full of warm, buttered popcorn.

"Want some?" she asks, holding a bag out toward me. "Wait, why do you look like you're going to cry? Did Lori say something? I knew—"

"No, Danny did."

She smiles softly at me. "Are they happy tears?"

"Yes." I quickly wipe them away. "He told me he couldn't because of his daughter."

"I knew it," she says, looking around to make sure no one can hear. "All these years, I knew that's the only reason he stayed with her. Remember how I told you about the time when Lori was pregnant and thought Danny and I had an affair?"

"Yeah."

"She told him that she would make his life a living hell and that he'd never, ever see their baby. That's why he cut off contact with you, Jennifer. He knew, if she ever found out, that's exactly what she would do. That's the kind of person she is. The truth is, when she filed for divorce, I immediately thought of you. But I was afraid, if Danny dated anyone while they were going through it, she would get vindictive. As it was, when they verbally finalized their settlement, she was the one who wanted out of their marriage, and Danny got what he wanted most."

"Custody of his kids?"

"Exactly."

"I respect him for that. Wait, when Phillip came in the house and saw me, he said you couldn't decide if you should contact me. If things were all under control as far as Lori went, why were you still hesitant?"

"Lots of reasons. You live in different cities. Danny could visit you in California, but he wouldn't move there. At least, not until the kids were done with high school. That's five more years. Logistically, there's a lot to consider. His kids. Your careers. For it to work, you'd probably need to be willing to move here. Or you'd have a long-distance relationship. Not to mention the fact that, at the time, I didn't know if you would leave Troy or work it out. I didn't want to see either of you hurt because I'd opened up some can of worms that I should have left closed, you know?"

"I know. And thank you for caring about me. About him."

Jadyn smiles back at me, but then her mouth turns down into a frown. I follow her eyes to see what causes it.

"Matt Malone," she mutters. "That kid is bad news. Dani shouldn't be talking to him."

"Why not?" I ask. "He looks cute."

"He thinks he's a badass," Jadyn replies. "Rides a motorcycle. Acts like he's all cool. I dated a guy like him in high school."

"Every girl needs to date a bad boy at least once, don't they?" I grin.

"Yes, but he's a senior, and Dani is a freshman. She's not ready for a guy like him, based on the way he's all over her."

"Should we go intervene?" I ask. "See if she wants to come sit with us? Have some popcorn?"

"Yeah, we probably should. Goodness knows, her mother won't do anything."

Before we can make a move, Chase comes out from the locker room with the team, sees Dani, and immediately steps in between her and Matt, taking Dani's hand and leading her across the field. Dani looks at Chase like he's her hero. And I can see why. Chase looks like the all-American dream boyfriend. His hair is messed up from playing. He's tall, and the pads under his uniform make him look much older than he is. If I were her age, I'd choose him over the bad boy any day.

"Chase to the rescue," Jadyn says.

"Has he ever considered modeling?" I ask.

"I don't think so, but maybe he should. He's always been photogenic."

"He belongs on an Abercrombie bag. He's kind of a little hottie."

"I'll have to tell him you said so." Jadyn laughs. "He will die of embarrassment."

My eyes get big. "Please don't tell him then. I don't want the kids to think I'm weird."

As we head back up the bleachers, Jadyn stops. "Lori's still here."

"Why wouldn't she be?"

"She usually only makes an appearance. She really doesn't like football."

"Does that mean she stayed because of me?"

"Probably. I should have kept my big mouth shut. Don't tell her anything. Like, *nothing*."

"You're still here," Jadyn says, sitting back down next to Lori. "Usually, you leave at the half."

"It's a gorgeous fall evening, and you know how I love football," she says, giving me a curt smile. "What about you, Jennifer? You a fan?"

"I love football," I answer honestly.

"So, am I to understand that you're seeing my husband now?"

"Seeing? Uh, no."

"He put his arm around you. In front of our children. In front of everyone."

"He didn't put his arm around me. Damon wanted to know my favorite pizza toppings. I guess we're going for pizza later. Is that a problem?"

"Considering we aren't divorced yet, I'd say so."

"Says the woman who was just showing off her engagement ring."

"What's that supposed to mean?" she snarls.

"It's not supposed to mean anything, Lori," Jadyn says. "She was simply stating a fact."

"Why are you here again?" Lori says.

"She's here because I invited her," Jadyn replies. "I might be working on a project in LA, and I needed her input."

"What kind of project?"

"An old hotel. She's the only person I know who has to deal with paparazzi out there, and that's a big concern for the new owner."

Lori reaches across Jadyn and sympathetically pats my hand. "You'll get used to it, honey. I deal with it *all* the time, being married to Danny. Although I bet, since your husband got caught cheating with all those women in Amsterdam—what did they call it? The Brothel Debacle?—that you have been hounded more than usual. The trick to having the press love you is never do anything stupid like that. But live and learn."

"Um, thanks, but he's not my—" I say as her phone buzzes.

"Oh, that will be Richard," she says, cutting me off. "We're off to catch our flight. Have a lovely weekend. I know I will. Sand. Surf. Amazing sex—something I wasn't getting at home. Ta-ta."

"Have a wonderful trip, Lori!" Jadyn turns, and whispers to me. "It couldn't have come at a better time. We won't have to see her until after the papers are signed on Wednesday."

Danny

I SHOULD PROBABLY say something motivational to the team as the second half is about to start, but I can't take my eyes off Jennifer. I can't believe I touched her back earlier, like it was the most natural thing in the world. The crazy thing is, that's how it felt. Natural. Like I'd been doing it my whole life.

The news that Lori is engaged should piss me off, but it doesn't. Especially when I watch Jennifer's backside as she walks up the bleachers. I love how she and Jadyn seem to be having fun together. My head is practically spinning from the thought of seeing her naked again as well as the future I wish I could have with her.

Phillip flicks me on the back of the head, getting my attention. "You're practically drooling."

"It's just so surreal. She's here. At my son's football game. She and Jadyn love each other. I should have—"

"No regrets—isn't that what you always tell me? She's here now; focus on that." He looks up into the bleachers. "Or on the fact that Lori didn't leave at the half, like usual."

"She and Dick Rash got engaged," I mutter.

"She's not going to like you dating Jennifer."

"I don't care what she thinks—wait. *Dating*?"

"You touched Jennifer in front of Lori. Was that to piss her off? Because you don't want to piss Lori off. You want Lori deliriously happy with Dick Rash until she signs on the dotted line."

"You think she will be mad?"

"She's a complete B, Danny. Of course she will. I bet she even cancels her trip."

"Speaking of that, did you know Chase offered to take my daughter to Paris on Saturday?"

"What? Why?"

"She was upset that Lori canceled on her for the spa. Chase said he'd do something with her instead. Said he'd take her in your plane."

"He wants her to be happy."

"I'm not sure I like that."

"Did you see what he did during the half? Did you notice how that senior was seriously hitting on Dani? How he had his arms around her? How Chase got her away from him?"

"No. What happened?" I say in a panic. "Who was hitting on her?"

"Matt Malone."

"I've heard he's trouble. Damon said he got kicked off the high school football team for fighting."

"That's him."

"He'd better stay away from my daughter."

"Oh, boy," Phillip says, causing me to shift my attention to the field. I assume we made a bad play, but the guys are just lining up for the snap.

"What?"

"Lori must have said something bad, based on the look on my wife's face. Oh, Lori's getting up and leaving."

"Do you think I should go check on them?" I ask.

"No, I think you should stay right where you are. Jadyn is a big girl, and she's been dealing with Lori's bitchiness for years."

"You don't really think Lori will cause trouble, do you?"

Phillip rolls his eyes at me. "It's all she's good at. When are you supposed to sign the papers?"

"Wednesday."

"You just have to make it until then. Lie low."

"Lying low with Jennifer sounds fun."

"That's the Danny I know and love." Phillip punches me in the shoulder and grins. "It's about freaking time."

OCTOBER 27TH

Jennifer

I SLOWLY WAKE up, coming out of a wonderful dream where I was with Danny on the field as he won the Super Bowl.

I half-expect the last few days to have been a nightmare, followed by a beautiful dream, but as I open my eyes, I see that I'm actually in Phillip and Jadyn's guest room in Kansas City. That, yesterday, I did see Danny for the first time in years.

Some things about the day were better than I could have imagined. Others times, it felt awkward. We had a great time after the game, eating pizza, talking, drinking a few beers. I had high hopes that he might walk me home and kiss me, but he simply muttered something about it being late and getting his kids to bed.

I close my eyes and remember how easily he slid his hand into mine when he showed me to this room. How his eyes drank in my nakedness. How he touched the small of my back at the game. How I longed for him to sneak over and touch me everywhere.

But the reality is, he's still married. I met his wife. Even though she left him and is newly engaged and happy, I got the feeling that seeing her husband touch someone else bothered her. And I can sympathize. I felt the same way when I saw the photos of Troy.

I don't want to hurt her. But I do want another chance with Danny.

I roll over and check my texts, hoping to find one from him. But then I remember he deleted my number a long time ago.

There are, however, numerous others.

Troy: *Please come home. I miss you. I need you.*

Troy: *Remember the song I wrote for you last time I was in rehab? I was just listening to it. I poured my heart into those lyrics, but they were all about me. About my struggles. My demons. I wanted you to understand. But I realized today that our relationship was too much about me. Going forward, it's going to be all about you. I'm going to spend my life making this up to you. If you will just come home.*

Troy: *Eddy, please come home.*

Me: *I'm surprised to hear from you. I hoped you would be in rehab. I'm sorry, but I'm not coming home.*

Troy: *I don't need rehab.*

Troy: *I need you.*

Troy: *I fell off the wagon. I've been mostly sober for years. It was just a mistake.*

Troy: *Please, baby, don't hold it against me. I love you. Always have.*

Me: *Mostly is the key word. It wasn't a one-time thing, and I can't do it anymore. I wish you the best.*

Troy: *That sounds like good-bye. Forever. Please don't say that. I can't go on if you don't love me.*

I don't reply.

My father always used to tell my mother that, if she didn't take him back, he would kill himself. Last time Troy went to rehab, he said I was the only thing that kept him alive. That is a huge weight to put on someone's shoulders. I told him so, but I didn't think he understood. The song lyrics he wrote *were* all about his struggle. I was *the light that shreds my soul.*

When I first heard it, I was actually offended. I didn't want to be a shredder of souls. But he explained it meant that my light shredded the darkness in his soul. He also seemed to think it was quite romantic. When he played the electronic mix version at clubs all over the world, he would dedicate it to me. And I always wondered if people thought that I'd shredded his soul rather than fixed it. If I was the cause of his darkness, not the light.

What I should have been thinking about was what being with Troy was doing to *my* soul. To my life.

I gaze into the facets of the beautiful little chandelier over the bed, determined to get my own sparkle back. I quickly get up, excited to start the day—and to see Danny again.

"I HOPE I didn't wake you," Jadyn says, covering up her phone's mouthpiece when I slide open the door separating the bedroom suite from her office. She's fully dressed and ready for the day, talking on the phone while poring over a mess of papers sprawled across her worktable.

"Oh no," I reply, looking down at my rumpled pajamas. "I was hungry. Thought I smelled breakfast."

"Breakfast was about an hour ago, but we saved you some. It's in the warming drawer under the oven. Go help yourself."

As I pass her desk, I notice the papers are an array of old photos, news articles, drawings, and swatches.

"Yes, I'm looking at that now," she says to whomever she's talking to. She pins a photo of an elegantly dressed couple who look like they walked straight out of casting in a 1920s movie to a large, empty bulletin board next to the table.

I make my way down to get some food, and when I get back, she's off the phone, and the board is half-full.

"What is all this?" I ask, picking up a swatch of a gorgeous teal paisley fabric.

"It's the history of the hotel in LA. I do an inspiration board for all my projects. As part of the purchase agreement, Tripp got the approval to tear the hotel down. My job is to design a new building. One that would be state of the art but still pay homage to its past. It's sort of what I'm known for. Mixing classic style and design with modern amenities. But I just had a call with the hotel manager and one of his valets who has been working there for over fifty years." She slides her fingers across a photo, pulls the pin out, and hands it to me. "This is Robert Lee Andersen. Everyone at the hotel calls him RL. His first month on the job in 1964, both Elvis Presley and Ann-Margret stayed there just after the release of *Viva Las Vegas*. This hotel has hosted every major film and recording star since the '20s, not to mention the big hitters in the industries.

"I know I'm going to lose the deal and a whole lot of money, but after talking to some of the staff and reading up on its history, I can't be a part of demolishing it. I always tell my kids, when someone says mean things, they are just trying to tear you down to their level. That they shouldn't allow it. That they should praise others, so they can rise higher together. That's what this job would be—tearing it down to level the playing field."

"I think you just summed up my life," I say, starting to get teary-eyed.

"What do you mean? I've followed your career. You're very successful."

"I make a lot of money, and I love what I do, but I just realized that my relationship with Troy has been nothing but a long series of tearing down and rebuilding. His reputation has affected my career." I glance at all the architectural drawings on the walls. "Did you design all of these buildings?"

"Yes. And every single one of them was a new build. Don't get me wrong; our company does renovations, but usually, they are just to make the inside of a facility more up-to-date and fresh for its employees."

"That was me. I'd swoop in, freshen up Troy's life, and then wait for it to fall into disrepair again. What do you think I should do? Raze my life and start over or—"

"Restore your beauty," she says. "From the inside out."

"What do you mean?"

"Do you think I've changed since we first met?" she asks.

"Well, sure. You've aged. Your style has changed. You're a mom. A businesswoman—"

"You're only taking into account my outward appearance and what I do, Jennifer. The person I am, my dreams, and the core of my being—those things have not changed. Neither has yours. You've just been covering them up on the outside. You're like this building." She points from a black-and-white photo of the hotel from when it was first built to one of it today. "See how the gorgeous arches got covered with awnings? Look at the tacky marquee for the bar that is hanging over an intricately carved door. And what about its European facade covered by a plastic banner proclaiming that you can stay in a room where a popular movie was filmed? We have to strip all that away and go back to what it was."

"Are you saying, I have good bones?" I ask with a laugh.

"And a good heart," she says, causing me to hug her.

"I don't want it all torn down," I cry out, emotions overtaking me. Even though I'm talking more about myself than the building.

I hold the hug for too long, but she doesn't complain.

Instead, she says, "Why don't you get yourself ready? Today is going to be a busy day."

"What are we doing?"

"I was going to turn the job down today, but you inspired me to rethink things. If I simply turn the job down, Tripp will hire someone else to do it. If we're going to save the building, I need to develop a renovation plan. While I do that, feel free to get caught up with some of your work things."

"I suppose I should at least call my agent and PR team and see how much damage has been done. They have been leaving me messages, all of which I have ignored."

"Perfect. You're welcome to make your calls in private, but feel free to use my office here. When I get in the zone, noise doesn't faze me. Danny will be at work all day, but Phillip is taking off early. The high school's homecoming game is tonight, and the parade through downtown is this afternoon. We're planning to meet for a late lunch, pick up the kids from school, and then go watch the parade. Danny doesn't usually get home on Fridays until around five. I'm going to throw something in the slow cooker on the way out, and we'll all eat dinner here before we go to the game. You're welcome to join us for any or all of it. I know you need some downtime, so I don't want you to feel obligated to do anything."

"Thanks. That sounds really fun. I'd love to go." Mostly because I want to see Danny again.

Danny

AFTER PRACTICE, I get in my car and head home. I kept Jennifer out of my thoughts as much as possible today, but it was hard. To be honest, I'm not quite sure what to do with her.

I wanted to text her last night after I got the kids in bed, but I deleted her number a long time ago.

When I get to my house, Melvin, the plumber, is loading up his truck.

I park, get out, and give him a wave. "How's it going?"

"Pretty good, man," he says, shaking my hand. "All that's left on the punch list is the install of the shower door. You can still use it. Just wouldn't turn on the steam. I'll start on the kitchen as soon as you make the final choices. So, how's the team doing? Gonna beat Denver this week? You know, I bet on you to win the big game this year. Odds at the beginning of the season were twenty to one. They're down to six to one now. And those Vegas boys know what they're doing; that's for damn sure. So, I'm just saying, you keep playing good, my two grand will become forty."

"I'll do my best."

Jadyn comes flying out of my house, obviously in a hurry.

"Great job, Melvin," she says to him, causing the tops of his cheeks to turn pink.

"Thanks, ma'am," he says.

After he heads out, Jadyn turns to me. "Phase one of your house makeover is almost complete."

"Remind me of what phase one is."

"Redoing all the bedrooms and bathrooms, your study, and workout room. I'd like to show you the tiles they finished around your tub, but we have to eat and get to the game. You're home late."

"Yeah, they were working on my shoulder."

Her eyes get big. "Did you hurt it again?"

"Not the throwing arm. My other shoulder is a little stiff. It got jarred on a tackle last week. Nothing unusual. Just got an extra-long massage."

"That's good." She blows out a breath of air. "You know Melvin's got two grand on you winning your third ring. I've got to get all the plumbing done in your house before the playoffs."

"Is Jennifer still here?"

"Yes. Why?"

"I'm just wondering when she's going home."

"Is that why you haven't made a move yet? You're afraid she's going home?"

"She was with the guy for about as long as I was with Lori. You don't get over that in a day."

"You do when it is the last straw," she argues.

"I've got enough going on in my life. I don't need to be jerked around by her. It's cool that she's here and all. It was really nice of you. And I will admit, it's great seeing her. But he's gone off the wagon before, and she always takes him back."

"Maybe that's because you were never in the picture before," she sasses. "I'm shocked, honestly, that you're not more excited by this."

"She's been here all of twenty-four hours! And I can't just make a move. I have to think about the kids."

"Danny, so help me." She stops in her tracks, turning toward me, the smile wiped from her face. "If you use the kids *again* as an excuse for not allowing yourself to be happy, I'm going to stop being your friend."

"No, you're not," I scoff.

She's been my best friend since the sixth grade.

"I. Am," she says, poking her finger into my chest with each word. "One. Hundred. Percent. Serious. Danny."

We have a staredown, neither of us allowing ourselves to blink. This is usually the part where she starts laughing.

But she doesn't.

"Fine," I say, giving in.

She gives me a happy smirk, grabs my elbow, and then drags me to her front porch. "Before we go inside, I'm just going to say one thing. Dani has the cheerleader sleepover tonight, and your son is spending the night at our house. You know, in case you wanted to have a sleepover of your own."

I gulp.

"Danny," she admonishes, "what's wrong with you? You told me that, if you'd slept with her when you first met, you wouldn't have left the bed for three days. You'll have to do with about twelve hours this time. Although I can keep the boys busy in the morning, Dani will be back home before her eleven o'clock spa appointment."

"You don't think it's too soon?" I ask.

"Soon? Are you kidding me? You've been waiting fourteen years for this!"

"It feels like a lot of pressure. Stop pressuring me!" I spit.

"Danny, calm down. There's no pressure. You don't have to invite her over. I'm just letting you know, I've opened up a window of opportunity. To use your terms, the offensive line is holding tight, and there's a crease in the defense. It's up to you to decide if you're going to keep the ball or hand it off to someone else."

"Very funny." I sigh. "I want to keep the ball."

"It's been a while. It's obvious that it's awkward for you both because of the baggage you're carrying behind you, but the sparks are still so evident. Invite her over. Go slow. Get to be friends. She needs a friend."

"I don't want to be her friend," I say adamantly.

"Yeah, you do. You always say you wish you had a relationship like Phillip and I have. He's my best friend. You and Lori were never friends. I want you to have it all next time around. I want you to feel hot passion, but I also want the woman you are with to really like you as a person. Love, friendship, and respect are important for a long, successful relationship."

"You've always said Lori doesn't respect me."

"She doesn't, Danny. And it kills me to watch."

"It sounds so old-fashioned." I smile and then give her a hug.

"Respecting someone has nothing to do with gender roles. There are guys on your team who you respect the hell out of, right?"

"Yeah."

"And are you friends with all of them?"

"Not like best friends."

"Respect means you value someone and their feelings. You appreciate them. Even when Phillip pisses me off and I think I hate him, I respect him enough not to do anything stupid. Not to say something in the heat of the moment that I would later regret. I respect him enough to always give him the benefit of the doubt. Even if he doesn't agree with me, I respect and value his opinion. I truly care what he thinks. He's smart." She smiles, wiggling her eyebrows. "Plus, he's hot. You are, too. At least you've still got that going for you."

I roll my eyes and walk into her house, which is surprisingly quiet. "Where is everyone?" I ask.

"I'm in the study," I hear Jennifer call out.

"Why don't you go chat while I do the final meal prep?"

When I don't move, she purrs in my ear.

"Shut up," I whisper, knowing what that means—she thinks I'm being a pussy.

I've never been nervous around *any* girl. Ever.

I take a deep breath, push my shoulders back, and walk toward the study with my normal cocky swagger. Like I'm walking out on the field for the biggest game of my life.

That is why I'm feeling nervous. It's been a long time since I've played this game.

"So, what did you think of the homecoming parade?" I ask Jennifer as I walk through the doors.

She's sitting in one of the big wingback chairs by the window with her feet tucked under her, looking like she belongs.

"It was really fun. The floats were cool, and I have a pocketful of Tootsie Rolls."

She pulls one out and tosses it at me. I snag it out of the air, unwrap it, and pop it into my mouth.

"Thanks."

"You can sit down if you want," Jennifer says, making me

realize that I've been standing here, chewing and staring at her.

"Oh, um, yeah." I take a seat.

She immediately gets up, shuts the doors to the study, and then takes her seat again. "Are you going to the game tonight?"

"Yes."

"And would you be okay with me going?"

"Sure."

"When we met, we were open and honest with each other. I know it's been a long time, Danny, but I hope that still holds true. So, I'm just going to lay it on the line. You broke my heart. And that sounds crazy. We spent a total of about forty-eight hours in each other's presence over the course of a few weeks and constantly texted each other in between. We tried to be just friends, and you were right to break it off. Now, you're getting a divorce, and I'm single. I didn't come here, expecting that we'd kiss and live happily ever after." She stops, shakes her head, and smiles. "Who am I kidding? That's exactly what I wished for. Because we only live once. And I think neither one of us has been living the lives we should have been. I want you to kiss me. I want to take things further. But I'm okay with getting to know each other again first."

"Jadyn suggested we get to be friends." I lean across the chair and then graze my hand across her cheek, almost like I'm checking to make sure she's real. "It's just that my life has gotten a lot more complicated."

"Dinner's ready!" Jadyn calls out from the kitchen.

I hear the sound of footsteps running up the stairs.

I hold Jennifer's gaze. "Will you sit by me at the game?"

She kisses me on the cheek. A slow, purposeful kiss that is surely meant to test my willpower.

"I'd love to," she says, pulling her lips from my skin. "Although should we be worried about being seen together? Like, does anyone even notice that stuff here?"

"Not really. Besides, we have a box."

"For a high school game?"

"Yeah, a lot of high schools pull in big crowds, and it's a way to get additional funding when they build the stadiums." I stand up and then offer her my hand.

I'm rewarded with the kind of coy smile that makes me want to completely skip the game. We might have changed over the years, but the spark and heat are still there, buried under the ashes.

Jennifer

WE QUICKLY EAT dinner, then load up in SUVs, and head to the game.

"People are tailgating?"

"We take tailgating seriously here," Danny tells me as the band marches out of the high school, leading a procession to the stadium.

"I'm going to hang out with my friends," Damon tells his dad and then quickly ditches us.

"And I'm going with him," Haley tells Phillip.

"Not so fast, young lady," Phillip says.

She rolls her eyes and then gives her father an angelic face. "I'm meeting Claire and Molly at the concession stand, and we're sitting together."

"That's fine, but I want you sitting and watching the game. Not running around." He pulls binoculars from his jacket pocket. "I'll be watching."

She huffs. "Fine."

Danny doesn't take my hand, but he does that thing again where he puts it across the small of my back and guides me through a private entrance to the suites. The suite is pretty basic, but it's heated, which is awesome. The wind is chilly, and I bet the metal bleachers would be cold to sit on.

"Jennifer?" a voice calls out. Very quickly, I'm being pulled into a bear hug. "How the heck are you? Saw the stuff you're going through when I was buying a lottery ticket. That Troy guy really fudged up this time. You leaving him for good?"

"Um," I say, feeling a little overwhelmed.

He releases me from his hold. "Heck, you probably don't even remember me. I'm Nick."

"Nickaloser?" I ask, causing him to turn a shade of red.

Jadyn starts laughing. He's even more handsome than when I first met him at a Nebraska game years ago.

"I haven't heard that name for a while—thank goodness," he says.

Jadyn wraps her arm around Nick's neck. "Also known as Kicky Nicky since he's a kicker. He got drafted to St. Louis out of college and then played for Baltimore, Denver, Atlanta, and Indianapolis but retired from football a couple of years ago. He's married to my sorority sister, Macy, and"—she points toward a couple of adorable children—"those are their twins, Kiley and Riley."

"Are you are just visiting?" I ask.

"No. Macy's family is from Oklahoma. Mine is from Nebraska. We decided to settle somewhere in the middle. That this one is here," he says, rolling his eyes toward Jadyn, "had no effect on our decision whatsoever. In fact, it was on the con side of the equation." He grins.

She gives him a sloppy kiss on the cheek, lets go of him, and runs off to pick up his children, covering their faces with kisses, much to their delight, based on their squeals.

"How old are they?" I ask.

"They're five," Danny replies for him.

Danny and Nick hug, and then Nick introduces me to his

wife, Macy, who quickly takes off to deal with a now screaming Riley.

"Why are you at this game?" I blurt out. I mean, it's a high school game.

"Another reason we chose Kansas City," Nick says, "is because Macy's sister lives here." He points down to the field. "That's her oldest son, Taylor. Number eight."

"Is he a kicker like you?"

"Yeah, kicker and punter. Plays soccer, too."

"That's awesome."

"Being around friends and family is what's awesome," he says sincerely. "We knew that, when our kids started school, we wanted them to be able to go to the same place and not have to move because of my job. Hey, are you going to be around this weekend? We're all getting together at the Mackenzies' on Sunday for a Halloween bash. Rumor has it, she's hired some local high school girls to keep the kids busy with face-painting and games while we drink."

Danny expectantly eyes me.

"Yes. I'll be here."

"Perfect," Nick says as the national anthem starts playing.

Soon, the home team runs through a large blow-up jaguar head and out onto the field.

"Oh, look at him!" Jadyn says. "I can't believe he's in a high school football uniform."

"I don't get it," I say. "Why is Chase out there? Isn't he in the eighth grade?"

"Kids have always been able to play up," Phillip explains. "Due to a couple of injuries, the high school team is short on quarterbacks, so they put him on the roster this week and are making him suit up. He'll probably never be on the field."

"Does he practice with them?"

"No, but the high school and middle school run the same

offense, so he knows the plays," Phillip replies.

"It's a big honor actually," Nick says.

"Except that he's going to hate it," Danny counters.

"Why would he hate it?"

"For an athlete who loves the game, sitting on the bench kills you. Not to mention, he'll be missing running around with Damon and their friends."

"Probably making out under the bleachers, like you used to," Phillip teases.

"You're one to talk," Danny teases him back.

Once we're sitting down next to each other to watch the game, I whisper to Danny, "You know, I've never made out under the bleachers before."

He gives me a grin. "Maybe, someday, we'll have to change that."

He takes my phone off the table in front of us, adds himself as a contact, texts himself, and then sends me a smiley face. And not just any smiley face. The one with the hearts in its eyes.

"There's Devaney," he says, pointing as the cheerleaders cartwheel their way over to their spot on the sideline. "She always looks so grown up when she's cheering."

The team does a choreographed stunt with Dani doing a series of back handsprings across the front of the squad.

"Wow. She's a good gymnast, too."

"That's because her daddy has spent a lot of money on private tumbling lessons," Danny says. "Competitive cheer is really—"

"Competitive?" I ask with a laugh.

"Exactly." He gives me a little elbow. "Smart-ass."

"You know it," I reply.

Nick leans in and whispers, "I'm not sure. Jennifer's ass seems more hot than smart, but if I tried to verify that, I'd probably get in trouble with my wife." He flicks Danny on the head as he gets up to get a plate of food. "I'll leave you to figure out which kind of ass she has, Danny. Report back tomorrow."

"Nothing is sacred around my friends," Danny says, shaking his head.

"I know. It's awesome how you all tease each other. It's fun but filled with love."

"They want to see me happy."

"And do they think I will make you that way?" I ask, trying to whisper so that no one hears this part.

"They already love you," he says.

And I can't help but wish he felt the same way.

"Well, the feeling is mutual," I say. "You're really lucky."

He glances back at his friends, all laughing, joking, cheering. "Yeah, I am."

Danny

IT'S INTRIGUING HOW seamlessly Jennifer fits in with my friends. In fifteen years of marriage, I never felt this relaxed. Lori tended to come off a little bitchy, and it could cause problems. Of course, no one really said anything about it, but now, they all act like they only tolerated her presence because of me, which is probably the case.

When the game is over, we head out to the car to meet up with the kids.

"Dani, you were amazing out there!" Jennifer squeals, giving Devaney a hug.

"Any chance you'd want to meet some of the team?" she asks.

"Devaney—" I start to say, but Jennifer cuts me off, "I'd love to!"

Devaney jumps up in the air. "Yay! Dad, did you remember to

bring my bag for the sleepover?"

"Sure. It's in the car. Do you need a ride?"

"Nope." She gives me a kiss on the cheek and whispers, "Thanks for letting me go. I promise I won't disappoint you."

"Good to hear."

She grabs Jennifer's hand and leads her over to where her squad is gathered.

"You should see your face right now, Danny," Jadyn says, sliding up next to me. She's patting the back of her youngest, who's asleep on her shoulder, while Phillip is talking sternly to Haley, who seems to want to go somewhere instead of coming home.

I smile bigger. "Do you think Devaney likes her?"

"She's a movie star. Her friends are going to go crazy," she says just as I hear girlie screeches coming from where Jennifer and Devaney are standing. "The more important question is, do you like her? She had fun at the game. Our friends love her."

"I know. It's kind of unnerving. Can someone just fit into your life so easily?"

"Maybe they can. So, if you and Jennifer want to ride home with Phillip, I'll wait for Damon and Chase. I'll be back. I'm going to put Madden in the car."

"Hey, Dad," Damon says, high-fiving me as he walks over. "Pretty good game, huh?"

"You look like you had a little too much fun," I say, wondering what's up with his ear-to-ear grin. More than likely, he did spend some time under the bleachers instead of watching the game. I decide to test him. "What was the play call on the passing score in the second quarter?"

"Double Fade from the Power I formation." He rolls his eyes.

"Where have you been?"

"In the locker room. Trying to talk my way onto the team."

"Did it work?" I laugh at my son's boldness.

"Well, I told Coach that he should probably have me suit up, too. Because, if Chase goes in, there's no one who can catch his passes better than me."

"Is that true?" Jennifer asks, rejoining us as the cheerleaders have dispersed and are loading into their cars.

"Definitely. I'm going back in the locker room. Chase and I will be back out in a few." He squints his eyes at Jennifer. "You gonna be here when I get back?"

"Um, maybe."

"Awesome. Saw you were taking pics with the cheerleaders. You cool with meeting some of the guys? Thought I'd sell tickets."

"Damon!" I chastise.

"Ah, Dad, I'm just joking. Well, sorta. I happen to know that Coach is a big fan of Jennifer Edwards. There might be a poster of her in his office. I was just thinking …"

"Go get in the car, Damon."

"I'd love to meet the coach," Jennifer tells him.

"Sweet!" he says, taking off.

"What did you decide?" Jadyn asks, sticking her head around the car.

"You guys go on home. We'll bring the boys."

"You know they're going to ask you to drive them through somewhere. Tell them I bought a big box of Hot Pockets just for them."

"We'll be home in a flash," Jennifer says, laughing. "I used to love those things."

When the Mackenzies pull away, Jennifer plops up onto the hood of my SUV like she owns it. "I'm surprised Damon doesn't play quarterback like you."

"He doesn't have the patience for it. He's fast, he has always loved to run races—well, win races—and he likes the glory of scoring. Even when they were little, Damon always wanted Chase to throw him the ball. Usually, instead of throwing it back, he'd run it back, hand it to Chase, and tell him to throw it again. And it's sort of how it worked out. They both love it, but they're young, and you don't know if they will grow into their positions. Chase is already tall, like Phillip was at his age, and expected to be at least six foot four. So, I think he'll be fine. The average professional quarterback is six-two. A couple of inches definitely helps with seeing over the offensive line."

"How tall is Damon supposed to be?"

"Since his mother's side of the family is shorter, it's harder to gauge but six foot probably. Six-one, if we're lucky. He's really fast, and he has soft hands. We're working with him this year on body control. He's actually taking some private ballet lessons."

"Ballet?"

"Yeah, pro wide receivers have to get two feet inside the field of play. They often go up on their tiptoes and drag them in bounds to make a catch. He won't be dancing, just working on balance, body control, and flexibility."

"Will Chase take ballet, too?"

"No, he has a throwing coach. Both boys go to national camps each summer. Colleges are looking at kids earlier than ever before, as are pro scouts."

"Will they go to Nebraska?"

"I don't know. They've had a string of coaches who haven't been winning, and recruitment is down. They just hired a former player as their coach, so we'll have to see how it goes. If your goal is to win things like the Heisman or to go high in the draft, a winning team helps get you attention. Although there are a lot of guys in the league who went to smaller colleges and do great in the combine. We just want them to get through high school with as few injuries as possible."

"It's funny how, when you watch a game, you don't think about how hard the players get hit. But when you got sacked in that Super Bowl game, I was worried."

"Jadyn always says she wishes Chase didn't like sports. She made him take piano lessons when he was younger. He hated it. He does like guitar though. He and Damon always say that rock star is their backup plan."

"I don't know about him being a rock star," she says slowly. "It's a different kind of life."

"Like being a movie star?" I ask.

She shakes her head. "Not really. With acting, you are mostly in a closed set environment. It's just you and the cast and crew. A rock star performs live in front of a whole bunch of people who are cheering, screaming that they love you, singing the lyrics you wrote. It's a big ego kick. Like, how could it not be?" She slaps my shoulder and starts cracking up. "Oh, Danny Diamond, what have I gotten myself into? I pretty much just described your job, too, didn't I?"

I move to stand in front of her. She instinctively spreads her legs out, giving me space.

"Yes, I perform in front of a lot of people, but then I take off my uniform, put on my suit, and go home. Where I'm just a normal guy."

"You've never been a normal guy," she says, sliding her hand into the back of my hair. She stares at me, her eyes dropping to my mouth.

I lean forward to kiss her.

"We're back!" my son yells out, interrupting what should have been a perfect moment.

He and Chase sprint over to us, Coach following behind them, sort of trotting.

"This is Jennifer Edwards," Damon says as Jennifer jumps off the hood.

After they share niceties and Jennifer offers to autograph the poster in his office next time she's at a game, we get the boys loaded into the car and head home.

It's only about a fifteen-minute drive. I have the music on and have my head against the back of the seat, straining to hear what the boys are talking about. I definitely hear the word *kissing* and the name of a girl in their class. Chase complains about being stuck on the bench.

Once I pull into the garage, the kids jump out of the car. Jennifer and I get out and stand awkwardly, staring at each other.

"What are *you* doing tonight, Dad?" Damon asks.

He and Chase are standing behind Jennifer, raising their eyebrows up and down at me. I swear, Phillip used to look at me the same way when he knew I was going to get some.

"Watching film probably and then going to bed."

The last thing I need is for Damon to say something to his mom. I don't want to give her any reason not to sign the papers on Wednesday.

I walk the three of them to the Mackenzies' front door and drop them off. "Night."

Jennifer doesn't look happy. When Phillip answers the door, before closing it on me, I can tell by the look on his face that he agrees with our sons. That I should be getting some tonight.

I'm not even back to my house when he texts me.

Phillip: *You. Are. An. Idiot. Who needs to grow a set.*

I let myself in my house, pace up and down the hall, and then decide he's right.

Me: *Any chance you'd want to sneak out?*

Jennifer: *Maybe ...*

My kids text all the time. Damon is always sending winky faces to some girl. But I realize I don't understand the subtle art of textual flirting. The younger guys in the locker room talk about it. Like what *dot, dot, dot* means. *Netflix and chill.* There are so many code words for hooking up. I suppose it's not any different than a girl who wanted to come over and *see my trophies* or any of the other excuses we'd make up when we only wanted one thing.

The problem is, I don't want just one thing from Jennifer. I want it all. And that's not something I can convey in a text. Especially when I don't even know how to tell her that in person.

My phone lights up with another text. I'm hoping it's from Jennifer, so I'll know what *maybe dot, dot, dot* means, but it's my daughter.

> ***Devaney:*** *We're at her house for the night. Thanks for letting me go to the sleepover, Dad. I really appreciate it. I'll text you in the morning.*
>
> ***Me:*** *Thanks for letting me know. Have fun. Love you.*

I jump at the sound of a knock.

When I open the front door, Jennifer's standing there. Apparently, *maybe dot, dot, dot* means yes.

Jennifer

"COOKIES," I SAY, holding out a plate. My cheeks are flushed from running over here in the cold, dark night. "Jadyn gave them to me as a bedtime snack. Thought you might want to share." I don't add *in bed*, but it's what I'm thinking.

"I'd love to," Danny says, grinning.

He leads me through the house to the kitchen. My head is on a swivel as I try to take it all in. To see where Danny lives.

He opens the fridge and takes out the milk. "Not spilling it this time," he teases as he pours us each a glass and then sits next to me at the island.

"These cookies are amazing," I say after taking a few bites. "What all is in them?"

"Natural peanut butter, vegan chocolate, gluten-free oatmeal, coconut sugar, cashews. For a cookie, it's actually pretty healthy."

"Is there anything Jadyn can't do? She makes motherhood and having a career look effortless."

Danny laughs. "She gets plenty stressed. Says baking relieves it. You know she's stuck on a project when she starts baking up a storm. Sometimes, in the middle of it, she just leaves the mess, walks away, and starts sketching. She's been working on my house along with her other projects."

I look around. The house seems very formal and a bit stuffy. Everything perfectly matched but not. The living room I passed was completely white with crystal chandeliers and a gold baroque wallpaper. The dining room was a bold pink and green, like a Lilly Pulitzer dress. The table was a gorgeous dark chestnut that you barely noticed in the midst of the matched drapery and chair fabrics. The kitchen I'm sitting in is white with glamorous, contemporary blue light fixtures dripping with crystals and a six-burner stove so shiny and clean, I wonder if it's ever been used. There are white quartz countertops, an elaborate blue floral arrangement on the counter, blue glass tiled backsplash, and a heavy fabric valance that mostly covers the view of the lake.

"Jadyn designed this?" I sweep my hand around, noting the attached family and breakfast room, which are done in an electric-blue-and-gold peacock motif. "That surprises me."

Danny starts laughing, almost choking on his cookie. He coughs, takes a big drink of milk, and then takes my hand. "I'll show you what we've done so far."

He leads me up an elaborately carved staircase and to a double door entrance. Based on its placement, I'm guessing it's the master suite.

I gulp. *He's showing me his bedroom. Yes!*

When he flings the door open, what I see is not what I expected. The paint is the color of sand, the ceiling the color of the sky. The bed in the center of the room is covered in a Bohemian print bedding. There's a desk with a furry chair.

"This used to be the master bedroom," he explains. "I just … well, after Lori left, I slept on the couch in the family room. I just couldn't be in here; the thought of her made me sick. Anyway, Jadyn noticed the dark circles under my eyes and got me to confess that I hadn't been sleeping in my bed in over a month. Of course, she marched over here, took a few measurements, and asked if I was ready for a change. If I wanted to make the house a place that fit me and the kids' tastes. The house had a guest suite on the main level, almost a second master, so we decided, since Devaney was getting older and she and Damon were already fighting over their shared bathroom, this would be fun for her. We got rid of all her little girl furniture, and Jadyn helped Devaney plan it all out. When she saw the chandelier in her bathroom, she was so happy, she cried. She has a big, private bathroom, a closet that she loves, and a sitting area where she can hang out with her friends."

"It's very cool. I bet she loves it."

"She took the divorce hard," he says somberly. "This sort of made it a perk. And the fact that Jadyn let her pick out a lot of the pieces herself made it that much better."

I take a peek in the bathroom. "Wow. This is massive. I love the chandelier, too, and the sparkly blue tiles."

"Those are new."

"Did she choose the bathtub, too?"

"No, that was here. I used it all the time even though it's too small."

"You take baths? I didn't think guys did that."

"Well, when your body hurts, a good soak in a warm tub before bed helps loosen up your muscles."

I have to bite my lip to get myself to stop imagining Danny

hurting and naked. How I would take care of him.

I'm snapped out of my reverie when he shows me a big closet filled with teen designer clothing and then takes me back into the hall.

He shakes his head. "I have no idea what kind of shape this room is in."

When he opens the door, I view a boy's room decorated properly with framed sports memorabilia and an oak furniture suite. Matching bed, dresser, desk, and a bookcase filled with more trophies than books.

"We didn't do anything to this room. He wanted to keep it the way it was. At first, I thought he was just trying to be a good kid, but then he told us what he wanted was a room that he and his friends could play video games in and how he wanted to decorate it the way he wanted. He pulled a stack of rolled up posters out of his closet that his mom would never let him hang on his walls."

We walk from the bedroom, through a Jack-and-Jill bathroom, and into another bedroom.

"This used to be Devaney's room. Chase and Damon helped Jadyn paint over the hot pink it used to be. She ripped up all the carpeting on this level and put in wood flooring. She bought them a big area rug and some gaming chairs, and then she gave them a box of thumbtacks and let them go at it. This is the result."

I take in the poster-filled walls. Everything from video games to sports heroes to girls in swimsuits.

"It's pretty awesome," I say because it is. "It also feels like a big *eff you* to his mom. What does your wife think about this?"

"Oh, she hasn't seen it. She would *not* be happy." He opens another door and shows me an inviting bedroom decked out in soft colors. "This is the new guest room. And, that's it up here."

"Do I get to tour the rest of the house?" I ask boldly, moving a little closer to him.

"Yeah," he says, "come on."

And I gladly follow.

"SO, THIS HAS always been my study."

"Oh, thank God. Finally, a room that looks like you," I blurt out.

"Like me?"

"Yeah. I just couldn't imagine you living in this house, kicking back and relaxing. I mean, I live in LA. I'm used to glitz and glamour, but the house felt stuffy. But let's talk about this room. The color is amazing. It's like a deeper version of your eyes. What did it look like before?"

"Well, it was done in a version of my team colors. The wood floor is the same, just stained a darker color. The windows were covered in a red, yellow, and blue check. The chairs were white with pillows that matched the drapes and had red fringe. The ottoman was a coordinating stripe. This is where I like to watch film. Turn on the fire. Lori wouldn't let me rearrange the furniture so that it faced the TV instead of the fireplace, so it was always a little awkward."

I take in the rich brown leather chairs, the houndstooth flannel ottoman, and the massive flat screen TV placed above the large wood fireplace. There's a rich blue-green color on the walls, which is offset by a rug in soft brown, gold, and blue tones.

"And look at this," he says proudly, opening an armoire. "Jay retrofitted the old TV cabinet into a bar. I have a little ice maker, my good scotch, and glasses right here."

I take in the bookshelf, running my hand across the spines of the hardcovers, noting the titles. "You like military, thriller, and spy books?"

"Yeah. Sometimes, I need a break from reading playbooks. I'm pretty sure, in another life, I was a spy."

"Oh, really? Although that doesn't surprise me. You have

charisma for days."

"Oh, you think?"

I take a step closer to him. "I most certainly do."

He sucks in a breath and backs away. Nods his head. "Um, I'll show you my room."

He slides his fingertips under a bookshelf, opens a hidden door, and directs me through. His bedroom is the same colors as the den, only softer. The bed features a gray tufted headboard and is centered in the room. The mattress is covered with high-thread-count sheets, a simple white comforter, and shams in a rich paisley. A deep blue throw rests at its foot. The walls of the room are dove gray with crisp white trim. It's both masculine and relaxing.

"I love your bedroom," I tell him. "I didn't notice any circles under your eyes. Does that mean you're finally sleeping?"

"Yes, I am. I spent a ton of time picking out a mattress. I ended up with a memory foam one that just molds around my body. The most comfortable bed ever."

"I've never tried one of those," I throw out, hoping he'll offer to let me in it.

Instead, he leads me into a wide hallway. "The bathroom was just completed today. Where my closet and bath are now used to be the guest bath and my wife's gift-wrapping room."

"She had a room for nothing but wrapping gifts?"

"Yes, she had rolls of wrap hung on little dowels and a whole lot of ribbons."

"The color of your study is so unique. And I can see that color is in your bedroom as well, just in a more subtle way. Did you pick the colors?"

"Actually, I sort of did. It was fun. Jadyn took me into my closet and asked me to show her my favorite suit and tie combinations. My two favorite pairs of shoes and one coat. She asked me if there was one piece of furniture, wall color, or item I'd want to keep, what it would be. I said the wood floors and a piece of artwork I bought a while ago that didn't match Lori's designs, so it was relegated to the garage."

"What clothing did you choose?"

We walk into a large closet, full of suits, workout clothing, and a combination of designer and athletic shoes.

"This navy pin-striped suit," he says, pointing. "This purple-teal-and-gray tie. My favorite brown leather jacket and a pair of brown suede Ferragamo driving shoes. Want to see the bathroom?"

"Yes!" I say a little enthusiastically, thinking about showering with him. But then I see a better alternative. "Now, this is a big tub!" I sit on the side of it and run my hand across its edge.

"It's got all the bells and whistles," he says proudly. "Massage jets, air bubbles. And my shower is big enough for my entire offensive line."

I can't help but laugh. "If you invited them all, you could probably sell tickets."

"What if I wanted to be in it alone, with you?" he jokes.

At least, he seems to be joking. He's chuckling. But that is not something to tease about. I don't know what to even say. *Do I joke back? Or do I strip naked and turn on the water?*

"I'm sure I would be amenable to that," I finally croak out then quickly change the subject. "I like what you've done so far. Are you redoing the whole house?"

"I am. It's funny. The house is sort of following my healing process. Originally, I told Jadyn to just change it. To do whatever she wanted. She chewed me out, big time."

"Because that's probably what you said to your wife, and you didn't love the result."

"Exactly. As a matter of fact, if you're still around on Tuesday, it's my day off. Like, if you'd want to hang out. But part of my day will be spent looking at new kitchen backsplashes, light fixtures, and dishes."

"That sounds like fun. I'd like to spend the day with you."

"Perfect," he says, pulling my hand to his mouth and kissing it. "I guess I'll finish with the tour."

And I'm thinking, *There's more? Why does there have to be more? Why couldn't it have ended in his bedroom? Or that tub?*

Danny

ALTHOUGH THERE IS nothing more I would like than to lock my door, throw Jennifer on the bed, and have my way with her, I find myself leading her down the stairs to continue the house tour.

Jadyn's right. I am a pussy.

"Where are we going?" she asks, looking forlorn.

"Uh, you haven't seen my favorite part of the house yet," I reply, showing off the home theater and bar.

It's surreal, having her in my house. Her shoulder-length blonde hair shimmers under the light, much like it did under the moonlight. I wish I could turn back time. But then I don't. I love my children and can't imagine a life without them.

"Oh, wow," she says upon entering my home gym. "This is like the shrine to Danny Diamond."

"Lori didn't want this *tacky stuff* in the house, so it had been in storage. Jadyn made me put it up on the walls. A lot of guys on the team have game rooms decorated with memorabilia, but I prefer it in my gym. I'm down here every single day, and it helps both motivate me and remind me of how far I've come."

She glides her hand along the chair rail, taking it all in, and it makes me nervous, like she's somehow inspecting my life.

"I have a little yoga room where I mediate and practice. This is like that for you. Your shrine to all things football. I take that back. It's your shrine to winning, to greatness."

"Not completely," I reply, leading her into the room that houses a sauna and bathroom. I point to the wall above the toilet.

"Tell me about this one," she says, taking in the photo.

My hair and uniform are soaked, clinging to my pads, covered in mud. My head is hanging low. Defeat written across my face.

"Divisional round playoff game six years ago. Played Pittsburgh at home. It was a grueling game, cold, messy. The weather ranged from rain to sleet to snow; the field was a wreck. I had the chance to throw a Hail Mary to a wide-open player in the end zone to win the game. I threw the ball too high. We lost. We were making a second championship run, and I blew it. So, it hangs over the toilet where it belongs."

"Yet you chose to hang it. Why?"

"Because I never want to feel like that again."

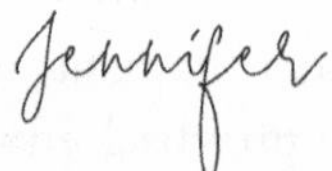

"DID YOU FEEL like that when you found out about your wife's affair?" I blurt out because that's exactly how I felt when I saw the video of Troy and those girls.

He blinks and then snaps his head in my direction. "Different," he mutters out. "It was more like a blindside sack. Something that seemed to come out of nowhere and knocked me on my ass."

"But did it really come out of nowhere? I mean, I felt that way with Troy, yet I had known it would happen again. How I found out—which was a call from my agent, who'd heard from my publicist—was awful. The way it spread across the internet was bad. My father is an alcoholic, and I swore, I would never be in a relationship with someone who had addiction issues. But I was. And I loved him. But he loved *it* more than he loved me. Plus, back when we first met, you weren't happy in your marriage. Did you get happy?"

"I would say that we had settled into a comfortable routine. The beginning of our marriage was rocky, but we worked out the kinks, learned to deal more effectively with each other, and I did love her. We have a beautiful family. People say no marriage is perfect, and mine was a prime example. There were things that pissed her off. I tried not to do them. We sort of carved out our relationship roles. As long as we followed those roles, our relationship was good. I haven't had a bad life."

"Me either," I say. "Just more downs than ups. Like Troy could be really sweet. He was creative and romantic, and that's a good combination. He made me feel loved most of the time."

Danny tilts his head in thought. I love that he's really talking to me about all of this.

"I think maybe that's the key. How much happiness do we deserve? When is wanting more wrong? Like, we both have high-paying jobs, doing what we love. We live lives others only dream about. We're blessed. So when you find yourself wanting more, that missing piece of the puzzle that would make your life perfect, you feel guilty. At least, I did. I felt like I should just be happy with all I had. So, even though Lori didn't end up being my dream girl, we made it work."

"I feel the same way. I had a rough childhood; we always had just enough but never any extra of anything. Now, I have so much. Sometimes, I wonder, *Why me?* And, when you have been given so much, asking for more does feel wrong, but I do want more. I've decided it's okay. We're similar, Danny. Our careers are golden. We love what we do. We're good at it. But just because we have so much in our professional life, doesn't mean we shouldn't strive for equal happiness in our personal life."

His blue eyes are transfixed on me, seemingly looking deeper, possibly into my soul, to see if I believe what I'm saying.

He takes a step toward me, possessively takes my face into his hands, and continues to look at me. He breaks eye contact for just a moment, his gaze shifting down to my mouth. He drags his thumb across my lower lip. I close my eyes as a soft moan escapes.

I tilt my face up, waiting for him to kiss me. Waiting for that perfect moment.

Instead, he drops his hands, walks back into the gym, and looks at the walls. "My wife was jealous of all this, I think."

I let out a disappointed sigh and then follow him. "I was with an international rock star and DJ, who also owns a production company that works with hot young stars. Truth is, I was never worried or felt jealous. Maybe that was a sign that I didn't care as much as I should have. All I'm saying is that if I were with you, I'd make sure girls knew I was your wife."

Why did I just say that? I can't believe I just mentioned being his wife. He doesn't want to kiss me. He's trying to bore me with a tour of his house, hoping I'll finally get the hint and leave.

I mean, we are here. No kids. No ties. No reason not to …

I follow him around a corner and gasp. "This is my favorite photo of you!"

On the wall in front of us is a mural of Danny holding Devaney with confetti raining down on them. On another wall is a similar version from when he won his second ring, only, in this one, he has both children in his arms. Both are equally touching. Even in a picture version, I can practically feel Danny's joy.

"So do I." He grins, leading me around a corner. "We took out the game room to expand the gym, which means this is my wall too."

"Why is it blank?" I ask. "I mean, every other wall is jam-packed."

Danny closes his eyes for a moment. When they reopen, they are moist, but he's wearing the same smile from the murals.

"What?" I say.

He grabs me around the waist and then turns me toward the wall, pressing his chest tightly against my back. Having him hold me like this feels like heaven.

"You know how people make dream boards to motivate themselves?" he asks.

"Like, with stuff they want to buy or places they want to visit?"

"Exactly. *This* is my dream wall," he explains.

"But there's nothing on it."

"That's because I visualize what I want it to hold. A third mural like the ones over there with confetti raining down, my children by my side, the fans cheering, the team going crazy, the pride and years of playing and practices, the injuries and pain, the pushing my body, the travel, and the missing my family—all culminated in one humbling, thrilling moment of victory. But when I just closed my eyes, I saw something different."

"What did you see?"

"You in the picture," he says, resting his chin on my shoulder.

I clutch my chest, my heart racing, then turn around to face him. "I'd love to be in that picture, Danny."

We gaze at each other. Both of us knowing what it means. That I want to be with him, share my life with him.

I kiss my index finger and place it on his lips then take my phone out of my back pocket.

Danny looks a little irritated, like I just ruined the moment, but I press a couple of buttons, and then I flip the phone around and show him that I have the same photo of him and Dani.

"I've had this picture in every phone I've had since it happened. I always wished—"

"That you were there with me?"

"Not just wished really, more like I felt like I belonged there but wasn't." Tears fill my eyes. I wipe them away and say, "I don't know why I'm crying so much. I mean, what the heck? How am I supposed to seduce you if all I do is cry? It's not very sexy."

"You want to seduce me?" He lets out a whoosh of air.

"I want to screw your brains out, Danny. Then I want to make love to you and have it be so freaking incredible that it wipes every other sexual encounter you've ever had in your life straight out of your mind. I want to win the Championship of Sex when it comes to you."

He presses his fingers against my cheeks, gently brushing away my tears. "I might have just fallen in love with you," he says.

"I'm pretty sure I fell in love with you that night on the beach," I confess.

I kiss him hard—a collision of lips, tongues, and entangled limbs.

He picks me up, carries me to a red leather sofa, and lies on top of me, bringing us even closer while never letting our lips part.

Finally.

I frantically run my hands through his hair as I arch my hips toward him.

A phone rings.

We ignore it.

But then it rings again.

He curses, ripping his lips away as he pulls his phone from his back pocket and looks at the screen. "It's Phillip." He presses answer and then says, "Yeah?"

I can immediately tell by the look on his face that something is wrong. He's already moving toward the stairs, leaving me lying here, like an afterthought.

Which sort of crushes me.

Because that kiss, just like our first one, was everything.

Danny

"YOU NEED TO get over here," Phillip says. "We just picked up Devaney from a party. She's a mess."

I panic, wondering what happened to her. How she ended up at a party. I start up the stairs and then remember Jennifer. Who I just kissed after all this time.

I turn around. She's still lying on the couch, her lips red from being kissed and her shirt partially unbuttoned with a sexy bra visible, looking incredibly gorgeous. How I would like to stay here and finish what we started. But I can't.

"Sorry, that was Phillip. There's some trouble with my daughter."

"But I thought she was at the cheerleading slumber party?" she asks, immediately getting up off the couch.

"All Phillip said was that she's a mess." I cover my face with my hand and rub my eyes. "I'm not sure I will be able to survive my daughter's teen years."

Jennifer takes my hand off my face and kisses it. "It's probably just girl drama."

WHEN WE GET to the Mackenzie house, I find my daughter on the couch in the living room, crying hysterically.

"What's wrong, honey?" I ask, but as soon as I get close to her, I can tell she's been drinking, and when she slurs her words and makes exaggerated hand motions, I know she consumed too much—which pisses me off.

"Where have you been?" I yell at her.

She cries some more, stringing together words that really don't make sense. She seems to be mad at Chase. I turn and notice him standing off to the side of the room with my son. Damon has a smirk on his face, like he thinks this is all funny, but Chase's face is red, and he looks as if he's been crying. Angel is clinging to his side, hating that Chase is upset.

I take two steps toward him. "What did you do?"

Phillip touches my shoulder, so I turn around, my face feeling like it's on fire.

"What happened?" I yell.

Even though my brain is telling me that Chase would never hurt Devaney, the anger I feel is overwhelming, and my daughter is clearly upset.

"Chase picked her up from the party," Phillip says. "That's why she's mad at him. I caught him and Damon in the garage, trying to sneak out. They were going to drive my car, go get her, and bring her home, so she wouldn't get in trouble."

I march over to my daughter and grab her hand off her face where she had it buried, and I start acting like a dad. "What were you thinking, going to a party? Why were you drinking?"

Devaney sobs harder then throws up all over the floor. And my shoes.

I hear Damon from behind me mutter, "That was awesome," as she drops her head into her lap and sings part of a song she liked when she was a little girl.

Chase, who has been stock-still in the corner, is next to her in a flash. He puts his arm around her, starts singing the song with her, and tells her it will be okay.

"I'll get that," Jadyn says to me, quickly getting up. "Don't move."

While Jadyn cleans up, I'm getting angrier and angrier. What the hell was my fourteen-year-old daughter doing, getting drunk?

I start in on her again. "You lied to me, Devaney. You are so grounded. Like, forever—"

Jennifer touches my back. "Now's probably not the time, Danny. I'd wait to have this conversation when you're not so upset and … when she's sober."

All of a sudden, Devaney looks up at Chase, like she just realized he was there. "Get away from me!" she yells at him very coherently. "I hate you, Chase Mackenzie!"

He gets tears in his eyes and quickly goes back to his corner.

Devaney starts sobbing again—about everything. Her mom not taking her to the spa tomorrow. About stupid boys. About how no one loves her. About cheerleading. About the divorce.

And I'm finding it hard not to sit down next to her and cry myself. *Does she really think no one loves her? That I don't love her?* I've spent the last five months since her mother left trying to make sure my children know how much they are loved. That our divorce has nothing to do with them. *Have I failed?*

Jennifer takes Chase's vacated spot on the couch. She pulls my daughter into a hug and starts rubbing her hair. She's speaking in a soothing tone and telling her over and over that everything will be all right. Devaney calms a little but keeps repeating the same things over and over. Almost like she's talking in her sleep.

While Jadyn finishes cleaning up the puke, Phillip grabs me and takes me outside.

"What the hell happened?" I ask as I pace across his front porch.

"Dani called Chase about a half hour ago. She was slurring, and Chase was really worried about her. He knew from some of his older friends that the cheer slumber party had turned into a huge, alcohol-filled blowout. Dani had texted him and was excited because it was her first high school party and because Dalton Michaels had been flirting with her. Apparently, he'd started texting her this week, but Dani was nervous about it because he had a date to homecoming with a girl on her squad. I guess Dalton kissed Dani, and the girl—who isn't his girlfriend, just a date—yelled at her in front of everyone and called her a slut. But what freaked Chase out and why he was willing to steal my car and go get her was that she said she was going to leave the party with Dalton, who had been drinking heavily."

"Jeezus," I mutter. "Then, what?"

"Chase told her not to leave the party. That he'd come get her. I caught him and Damon in the garage. Chase spilled everything he knew, begged me to drive them. I did. There were cars lined up and down the street. I told Chase I was going in with him, but he said no. A couple of minutes later, he texted to tell me to call the cops and then pull up as close as I could to the door because he'd be out in sixty seconds." Phillip smiles proudly. "Damon timed him. It took forty-seven. He had gone in there and found her with Dalton, who was drunk and all over her. Chase said something and pulled Devaney away. Dalton threw a drunken punch. Chase ducked, and Dalton's hand smashed into the stone fireplace instead. Chase said he heard bones crack. Anyway, he got Dani out to the car, and we got the heck out of there."

"So, Devaney is mad at Chase because he rescued her? He kept her from getting into a car with someone who would have been driving drunk?"

"Yeah, that's why he's so upset."

I shake my head. "I'm not ready for this. How are we going to survive high school?"

"We survived it the first time around," he says with a grin. "Dani is safe. That's the main thing."

"She's drunk as a skunk."

"She's drunk, but she was walking okay, and we did get her to drink some water in the car. If I'd thought she had alcohol poisoning, I would have taken her straight to the hospital."

I take a deep breath. "Thank you," I say sincerely.

"You'd do it for me," he says back. "But I'd appreciate it if you apologized to Chase. He looked horrified when you asked what he did."

"I'm sorry. You're right. I'll do that and then take my daughter home."

Jennifer

DEVANEY IS FINALLY mostly asleep. Every once in a while, she wakes up, sobbing. I'm glad that she threw up and got some of the alcohol out of her system. It's kind of ironic that I ended up here because of alcohol, and now, I'm consoling Danny's sweet and way-too-young-to-be-drinking daughter over it.

I guess at least I know that you can't have a sensible conversation with someone who's been drinking and that it's important to keep them calm.

The front door opens, causing me to look up and into Danny's eyes. They look exactly like they did in the photo of him above the toilet. Defeated. I give him a faint smile, trying to let him know that it will be all right.

He goes over and speaks quietly to Chase then sits on the other side of the couch, next to his daughter. "I'm going to take her home now," he says.

"Do you want me to help you?"

"No, you've done enough already."

I should take that as a nice thing for him to say. Maybe it's because he's upset, but the way he said it makes me feel like, if I hadn't been making out with him on his couch, none of this would have happened.

Very quickly, he and Devaney are out the door.

I walk into the study off the kitchen and sit in my favorite chair, curling my feet up underneath me, the evening we spent together still on my mind. Angel comes into the study and lies at my feet. Usually, she doesn't leave Chase's side when he's home, but she looks as exhausted as I feel. I lean down and rub her ears. She pushes her head against my hand, like she loves it. Pretty soon, she's rolled over and letting me rub her belly.

From my perch, I can see Jadyn sitting down at the kitchen table with Chase.

"You know you're grounded," she says.

"But, Mom—" he argues.

"Chase, what you did tonight was good, but if your father hadn't driven you, it could have gone very badly. I applaud the fact that you wanted to keep her from going with someone who was drunk. I understand you had good intentions. But you're fourteen. You don't have a license."

"I told him it was a bad idea," I hear Damon say.

"Damon, why don't you go downstairs and sleep on the couch tonight?" she replies in a serious tone.

"Yes, ma'am," he says.

"And, Damon, don't forget, you were in the car with him, too."

I see him walk by the study, on his way to the basement stairs.

"She's trying to fit in. To be cool, Mom," Chase says. I feel bad for him. "I don't understand. She's already the coolest girl I know."

Phillip walks into the study with an open bottle of wine and three glasses. He pours a glass, hands it to me, then pours one for himself, and sits in the chair opposite me.

"If Dalton broke his hand, he's going to hate me because I'm a QB, too," Chase goes on. "What if I take his—"

Phillip sighs, gets back up, and shuts the French doors. "I'm going to give them some privacy," he says. "How are you? This is a lot to cope with."

"We haven't toasted yet. Can I drink?"

Phillip smiles at me. "You're getting the hang of it. Well, let's see. Why don't you do the honors? My brain is fried."

"Here's to your children being safe and to Danny's empty wall." I clink his glass and then take a sip of a bold red.

Phillip looks at me kind of funny, but he takes a drink and then grabs a remote to turn on the gas fireplace. Angel wags her tail at him, so he gives her a quick pat and then sits back down.

"Oh, that's nice," I say. "I love this room. It's so cozy."

"It's Jadyn's favorite, too. And the only room in the house that is off-limits to the kids, which might be why." He laughs. "So, explain why you're toasting to an empty wall. I take it, you went over to Danny's house tonight even though you said you were tired and going to bed."

"I was going to bed," I say quickly, feeling like I got caught lying and sneaking out, too. "I mean, originally, I'd been hoping he'd invite me over. But he didn't. I was a little sad about that, so I was just going to go to bed. He texted me when I got to my room."

"I told him he was an idiot for not inviting you over. So, did you have fun?"

"Probably not the kind of fun you are referring to, based on your grin," I say with a laugh.

"Seriously?" Phillip slaps his palm to his forehead and rolls his eyes. "What did you do then?"

"He gave me a tour of his house. Showed me the changes that have been made so far. It was fun. We talked a lot. And it was really interesting to see how the parts of the house that had been redone were so different from the ones that weren't."

"Lori wanted their house to be a showpiece."

"It was fun to see Danny in his study. He seemed happy there. But then he took me to his gym."

"His favorite place."

"I suppose. It's like a shrine to his greatness," I counter as the doors open, and Jadyn joins us.

Phillip gets up immediately and pours her a glass of wine.

"I so need this," she says. "What did you two toast to?"

"To the kids being safe and Danny's empty wall," Phillip tells her.

Jadyn squints her eyes at me as she and Phillip snuggle up together in the chair.

"And Jennifer was just about to tell me why. Danny invited her to come over tonight and gave her a tour of the house. She likes what you helped him do so far."

"And we were talking about his gym," I add.

"Did he tell you what the empty wall was for?" she asks, quickly coming up to speed.

"Yes," I say with a smile, taking another sip of wine.

Regardless of how the night ended, he told me that I belonged on his dream wall, and that made me feel incredibly happy.

"Oh, boy," Phillip says, eyeing my dreamy state. "I think I'm going to leave the rest of this conversation to you ladies. I need to go talk to Chase now that he's settled down a little." He finishes the rest of his wine, kisses his wife, gets up, then grabs the bottle, and sets it on the table between us.

"He's up in his room," Jadyn says. "Be gentle on him. He's had a rough night."

"I know he has. That's why I want to talk to him. Even though he's grounded, I'm very proud of him. I want to be sure he knows it." He gives Jadyn an adorable wink, gets Angel to come with him, and then closes the door behind himself.

"Sorry you had to deal with all this tonight," she says. "You did really well with Dani."

"I've had my fair share of dealing with drunk people," I reply.

She takes another drink of wine and then says, "So, tell me about the wall."

I sit up straighter. "You know it's his dream wall, right?"

She nods.

"He told me about how he wants another picture like the ones with his kids."

"And?" she prods.

"He said, when he closed his eyes, he envisioned me in the picture."

She leans her head back into the chair, closes her eyes, and sighs.

"What?" I ask. "Is that good or bad?"

"Oh, that's very good. While he might call it his dream wall, it's more like a concrete goal for him. He wants to go out on top."

"You think, if he wins the big game this year, he'll retire?"

"I think maybe so. His body is still in pretty good shape—"

"I'd say so. Have you seen his underwear ads?"

Jadyn lets out a laugh. "Yes, I have. Danny has a very nice physique. I was referring to the fact that he's not had many concussions or injuries. Football can be hard on the body even if you're in top shape."

"Makes sense." I take a sip of wine, contemplating whether or not I should even ask the question I'm considering. Finally, I blurt out, "Is Danny really not good in bed?"

"What makes you think—oh, wait, Lori said something like that at the game, didn't she?"

"Uh-huh. I want to know what you know."

"Well, I've never slept with him, but you've seen him play football. You know how passionate he is."

"Why would his wife say that?"

"Trying to make it look like she traded up when she didn't. Trying to make you think that, so you wouldn't want to sleep with him."

"Was their sex life bad? Like, I can't even imagine it ever being anything but amazing with him," I gush.

"Maybe you'll have to find out for yourself," she teases. "But, to answer your question, it was good between them at first. Danny never would have married her otherwise. It went downhill when she was pregnant, and then it came and went in waves."

"Like an orgasm," I screech out. Maybe I should stop chugging wine. But then I whisper, "He kissed me."

"Based off the kiss, what do you think?"

"I think it would be incredible."

OCTOBER 28TH

Jennifer

I HAVE TWENTY-SEVEN missed calls, numerous voicemails, and a litany of texts from Troy when I wake up. I listen to the first voice mail and can tell that he was drunk. Again. I delete the rest. I'm not going to deal with it. I send a quick text to his manager, letting him know that I am not getting back together with him and that he needs to get Troy to rehab fast. That he'll self-destruct otherwise.

My phone buzzes in my hand, only this text is not Jason replying.

> **Danny:** *I enjoyed spending time with you last night. Not exactly the way I'd hoped the night would end. I'm sorry you had to deal with all that.*
>
> **Me:** *She's 14. Stuff like that happens.*
>
> **Me:** *Wait, how did you hope the night would end?*
>
> **Danny:** *I was hoping it would never end.*
>
> **Me:** *That might be the most perfect answer ever.*
>
> **Danny:** *I'm getting ready to leave for work. I'm in my driveway.*
>
> **Me:** *Okay. Cool.*

My phone immediately rings.

"I sound like a stalker when I text you," he says when I answer. "I have a few minutes before I have to leave, and I was wondering ..."

"Don't waste time talking, Danny. Get your ass up here," I say, hanging up, jumping out of bed, and running to the bathroom to brush my teeth. Thankfully, I always take my makeup off before bed, so I don't look like a complete mess. Well, except for my hair. But who cares.

I'm spitting out toothpaste when I hear a knock. I drop the toothbrush, wipe my mouth with the towel, and race to the door.

"You're not naked this time," he says, giving me a once-over. "But I don't mind at all."

I glance down at the skimpy nightie I'm wearing. One that Jadyn bought. "I was in bed when you called." His eyes wander in that direction along with my mind. "When exactly do you have to leave?"

He reaches out and touches my shoulder, gliding his hand across it and down my arm. Shivers race up my spine.

"Do you have plans for tonight?"

I glance at the bed again. I can't help it. I swear, I can't think when this man touches me. I couldn't back then, and I can't now.

"Um," I stutter.

"I'll be home from practice around five. I was wondering if you'd like to have dinner with me."

"More pizza with the family?" I ask.

He doesn't reply, just lets his fingers skip to the skinny strap of my nightie, teasing me. He lets go of the strap, moving his hand to my face.

He briefly presses his lips against mine, and then he's gone.

I touch my lips, wanting to hold the kiss in. When I hear the door shut, I rush to the window so that I can watch him walk away.

Phillip and Jadyn come out the front door, dressed for a run, as Danny comes around the corner of the house and across their driveway. He stops and talks to Jadyn. I'm not sure what they are talking about, but he glances toward my window as the conversation appears to get heated with Jadyn gesturing big. Danny soon throws his hands up into the air and walks off, getting into his car and leaving.

Jadyn turns to Phillip and appears to be ranting. He grabs her face in his hands and kisses her, very effectively shutting her up. When he stops kissing her, she grins at him and then swats his butt, and they take off on their run.

I move away from the window and sigh dreamily at their display of affection.

But then I wonder if they were arguing about me.

And I probably shouldn't, but I keep thinking about Dani and how she was crying last night. I put on some clothes, twirl my hair up into a bun, traipse over to their house, and ring the bell.

It's then that I realize it's early, and she's probably still sleeping it off. I'm surprised when she quickly answers the door.

"Hey," she says, letting me in.

"Hi. I, um, look, I know you don't know me."

"You hugged me last night and whispered sweet things to me," she says. "Thank you."

"I wasn't sure if you'd be up."

"My dad slept on the floor of my room last night. He was worried about me. And mad."

"You scared him," I reply. "And lied. It felt like a slap in the face to him. Especially with some of the things you were saying."

"That no one loves me?"

"Yeah."

"I know my dad loves me. It's just … the divorce and cheer and school. Sometimes, I feel like a big loser. And tonight is homecoming, and I have no idea what I'm going to do."

"Well, that's the reason I'm here. Are you grounded?"

"For three weeks or until the end of my life, whichever comes first," she says in the dramatic way only teens can. "Dad woke me up before he left to let me know that. He was nice and made if effective starting Sunday, so I could still go to the dance. Part of me wishes I were grounded tonight, so I wouldn't have to go."

"Why don't I make some breakfast, and we can talk about it?"

"You like my dad, don't you?" she asks.

"Um, yeah, I do. But I don't know if he likes me back."

She rolls her eyes again as we walk into the kitchen. "Boys."

"Tell me about it," I tease as I open the fridge to survey its contents. "But I'm not here because of that. Last night, the things you were crying about. I felt your despair. And I've been there. My parents got divorced when I was young. It was rough."

"Really? All my friends act like it's no big deal. But it is. Everything in my life is changing all at the same time, and sometimes, I feel like I can barely deal, you know? First, I make varsity. There were parents who got all pissed off. Acted like I only made it because of my last name. They bring judges in who don't know our names, only our numbers. Our tryouts are judged like a competitive event. Top scores make the first team, and second set makes JV. I've taken gymnastic classes and been cheering competitively most of my life. I'm the best tumbler on the squad. But there was all sorts of drama. And half of the seniors hate me because a couple of their friends didn't make it this year."

She stops to take a breath when I hold up my finger.

"Waffles, pancakes, or French toast?" I ask. "There's cinnamon bread in the pantry. I'd vote for the toast."

"That sounds really good," she says. "Is there bacon? And do you want me to help you?"

"No. You keep talking. I'll listen and cook."

"So then," she says, apparently agreeing, "my parents decided to get a divorce. Of course, I'm not allowed to tell anyone about it yet, which sucks. Dad doesn't want the media stuff that will follow. I mean, we're the perfect family."

"Do you not like that?"

"I'm not perfect." Her phone buzzes again. It's been buzzing off and on since I arrived.

"Do you need to get that?"

She picks up her phone, glances at it, and then sets it back down. "I can't deal with it right now. Last night was such a disaster. The thing is, I didn't lie to my dad. I did go to the sleepover. A few guys crashed the party. Next thing I know, there were a whole lot of people there. Then, there was drama because of this guy."

"The quarterback? What's his name?"

"It's Dalton." She gives me a wry smile. "He's really cute and a senior; it's hard not to like the attention."

I'm dipping toast into an egg wash when it suddenly hits me, how hard parenting is. "Um, Dani, here's the thing. You don't date a guy for the attention." But then I think about myself. "Yet I did it myself."

"With who?"

"Troy. He showered me with attention when we first met. He was handsome. A freaking rock star. It was flattering."

"Yeah, but you are an actress. You're famous, too," she counters.

"To you, I might be. In my head, I'm still a tomboy with big lips. My dad was an alcoholic and not the best influence on my life. I get wanting attention for attention's sake. Some of us seek it. But it always seems to come at a price."

"Like Amsterdam?"

"Yes, exactly." I put some bacon in a pan to fry while I pour a little batter on the stove's griddle to see if it's hot enough yet. I take a sort of perverse pleasure out of getting this spotless stove dirty. "There's a difference between liking someone because of the attention you get as a couple versus liking someone because he's an awesome guy who treats you well."

"My dad treated my mother well. He was also so patient with her, even when she was a bitch, but she still left him." She puts her head down and traces her finger on the counter. "I'm pretty sure my mom had an affair with Richard. And it bothers me that no one will just tell the truth."

"Maybe they think you're not old enough for the truth. What makes you think they were having an affair?"

"Because her story doesn't add up. She told us she met Richard—he's her plastic surgeon—and they became friends. She says they just had this attraction, and she couldn't stop thinking about him. That life is too short to live without that kind of love."

What she says makes my heart hurt, knowing that I could have given her father that kind of life. "I agree with your mother on that," I say as I flip the bacon and start cooking the French toast.

"Except she just decided to up and leave my dad after fifteen years because she couldn't stop thinking about some guy? Who does that? Plus, she moved right in with him. If they were just getting to know each other, she would have gotten her own place. There's a photo of them together, kissing, at their house. Her hair is colored in a way it was before they separated. So, something was obviously going on."

"Does it really matter?" I ask her.

"Yes, it does. Because, eventually, it's all going to come out in the press. And then my friends will hear about it. Really, I'm shocked my parents have managed to keep it a secret for as long as they have."

"Doesn't your best friend live next door?" I ask gently.

She's yet to bring up her fight with Chase.

"He's like my dad! He doesn't want me to grow up either. And he's just jealous because of Dalton."

"Because Chase likes you?"

"It's not like that. I mean, it's sort of like that, but we're friends. He's my best friend—well, *was* my best friend."

"He rescued you from the party last night. It was obvious that you had him scared. And you were going to get in a car with someone who had been drinking a lot." I get the syrup out, load French toast and bacon onto two plates, then set them on the bar and sit down next to her.

"This looks really good," she says, digging in.

"You feeling okay this morning?"

"Yeah, Dad said the one good thing about last night was that I puked. Although I owe Auntie Jay and Uncle Phillip apologies, too. And probably everyone else in my life, who I don't want to face." She points to her phone, looking forlorn. "He hasn't texted me. He always texts me."

"Dalton?"

She shakes her head. "No, Chase. And I know he's up because my brother was texting me to find out how much trouble I got into. Telling me that he's mad at me because he and Chase were supposed to go to some eighth grade girl's spin-the-bottle party tonight, and I ruined everything. Chase must have gotten grounded."

"Well, he did sneak out of the house and was going to steal his dad's car. He looked pretty distraught last night." I wave my fork. "Especially when you said you hated him."

She lets out another sigh. "I'm supposed to go to the spa today. Would you want to come with me?"

"I thought Jadyn was going?"

"I was thinking maybe you could tell her that you wanted to go instead?"

"Chicken," I tease.

"Totally," she agrees, smiling at me.

"When you do that, you look like your dad."

"When I smile? Yeah, everyone says that."

"How did you end up with Dani as your nickname?" I blurt out something I've been wondering since I got here.

"When Chase tried to say Devaney when he was little, it came out as Dani. He and pretty much everyone but my parents have called me that since." She lets out another dramatic sigh, probably thinking about how she treated Chase last night. "So, what do you think?" she asks as her phone buzzes again and again.

"I'll go with you. But only if you don't take the phone." She nods her head, but then I say, "And you go apologize to the Mackenzies first. *All* of them."

"Never mind," she mutters.

"What time do your appointments start?"

"Eleven."

I glance at the clock on the microwave. "That means we have about an hour to fix things." I take her phone off the counter and hand it to her. "Read them to me. I'll help."

She takes a last bite of toast and pushes her plate aside.

"Okay. Be brave, Devaney," she says to herself as she starts scrolling. "First up is the cheer captain. It's a group text to the squad. She's freaking out that she's going to get kicked off the squad because the cops showed up at the party. And she's mad at the two girls who started the party to begin with."

"Was she drinking?"

"No, she was freaking out the whole time, trying to get people to leave. Her parents were due home in a few hours. She's also basically grounded for life."

"Do they expect you to reply to the group text? Did they mention your name?"

"No."

"Then you don't need to reply. If your cheer coach asks on Monday about the party, tell her the truth about who invited the guys and how it got out of control. It's shitty, what her friends did to her."

"I can do that. Hmm. I have some other random texts from people about the party. Mostly from people who weren't there, wanting to know if the rumors are true." She keeps scrolling, and her phone keeps vibrating. "Oh, no."

"What?"

"Apparently, the cheer coach found out and called everyone's parents. Everyone is getting grounded and … *ooh* … Dalton's date just sent a text in big bold letters, saying that she's grounded and that her parents won't let her go to the dance tonight."

"And has Dalton texted you?"

"Yeah. He broke his hand. His throwing hand. He'll be out for the rest of the season. Idiot."

"Idiot?"

She rolls her eyes. "Or I'm probably the idiot."

"Maybe you should tell Chase that."

"He offered to take me to Paris today," she says dreamily. "When he found out my mom had bailed on me."

"We'd probably have a much better time at the spa if you apologized to him first. Why don't I clean up while you go over there?"

"Okay," she says, rushing toward the door. She stops, turns around, and flashes a smile in my direction. "Thanks, Jennifer."

Danny

I WAS PISSED off when I left for work, mostly because I knew Jadyn was right. And I hate that.

On the way home from practice, I call Marcus, a former offensive lineman who retired after we won our second ring together, to get a second opinion.

"What's up, my man?" he asks. "My wife and I are dressing as superheroes for the party at the Mackenzies' tomorrow. I'm the Incredible Hulk. How about you?"

"I'm going as a professional football player," I say dryly. "That's not why I called though. I need some advice."

"Lord have mercy, tell me it's about a woman," he practically squeals. "Who is she?"

"Lori and I have agreed verbally on everything. Wednesday, we meet to sign those documents and submit them to the court."

"Thank goodness. Knowing this secret for months has been killing me."

"Whatever. Anyway, there's this girl I asked out for dinner tonight. But Jadyn told me I shouldn't take her down to the Plaza because, if people saw us together, rumors would start. People would think I was cheating on my wife. It'd be a mess. Plus, she's kind of famous, too."

"Is it Jennifer Edwards? Holy shit, dude. I heard she was staying at the Mackenzies'."

"Yes, it is. Now, I don't know what to do. I promised to take her out."

"If I were dating that fine woman, all I'd want to do is stay in—her," he says, with a laugh.

"So, you think Jadyn is right?" I ask, ignoring the sexual comment.

"Yeah. Order food. Set it all up pretty in the dining room. Serve her dinner, *naked*."

"I was thinking maybe a picnic in front of the fireplace. There's a chance of snow tonight."

"That'd be good, too. As long as you're naked."

"You don't think Jennifer will think it's lame? We haven't seen each other for years. I can't meet her at the door, naked. I just don't want her to think staying in is boring."

"I would hope, if you're naked, boredom wouldn't be an issue," he says with a laugh. "But I get what you're saying. So, definitely set it up pretty in the dining room. Make it feel special, and it will be. Get her some flowers. Remember all that stuff you used to have to do in order to get laid?"

"Like buy diamonds?" I quip.

"I'm not referring to your soon-to-be ex-wife. I'm talking about *before* you were married."

"I'm pretty sure I just smiled in a girl's direction back then."

"Figures. You've always been a pretty boy." He starts talking in a singsong voice, "I have your underwear ads taped up in my gym. Hashtag goals."

"Very funny."

"You want to see funny? If you aren't careful, I might just steal that Jennifer away from you."

"Somehow, I don't think Madison, your wife, will allow that." I chuckle.

"No, you're right. That woman still has me wrapped around her little finger. Not to mention, she looks damn fine dressed as Wonder Woman. Hoping to get her to wear the costume to bed. See you tomorrow."

I HANG UP and immediately call the restaurant where I wanted to take Jennifer. It's a barbecue joint, but it's a nice place. Plus, they have cheesy corn worth splurging on. I order food and then stop to pick up flowers and champagne. When I'm at the floral shop, I realize the last time I was here was the day Lori told me she wanted a divorce.

"It's good to see you, Mr. Diamond. Usually, your wife comes to pick up your order. It's so sweet that you buy her flowers every week."

The florist goes back to a cooler and brings me a container full of the flowers I always got for Lori, and I realize that Lori has been sending herself the same flowers every week since then, probably to keep up appearances.

No freaking way will I be taking those flowers home.

"What do you have that's a little different?" I ask.

"Well, with Halloween parties and homecoming tonight, we've been mostly focused on that. Lots of mums and fall colors. Your wife prefers more exotic blooms."

"Can I see what my options are?"

"Sure," she says, leading me into a huge cooler. "Take your pick."

"These," I say, pointing to a container of roses. "A couple dozen." I walk back out and see all sorts of fun Halloween decorations lying on a worktable. "Can you include some of this stuff, too? I want it fun and gaudy. Something my wife wouldn't like."

"Uh, sure," she says, looking perplexed. "Give me a few minutes."

About twenty minutes later, she comes back out with a large container. "I covered it all up. You'll have to wait to see it until you give it to her. If your wife hates it, please don't mention where you got it."

"It's not for my wife," I say, causing her to look aghast. "Uh, they are for my neighbor, Jadyn Mackenzie. She and Phillip are having a Halloween party."

"Oh! You should have told me that. Wait! I'll be right back." Ten minutes later, she comes back with an even bigger wrapped vase with orange and black balloons filled with glitter trailing behind it.

"It's a masterpiece," she says. "Have you picked out your costume yet?"

"No. Any ideas?"

"It's funny really. So many kids in Kansas City want to be you for Halloween. What did you want to be when you were growing up?" she asks.

"A football player," I reply without hesitation as we finish our transaction.

BUT AS I'M driving home with the vase buckled into the front seat next to me, what she said is on my mind. *What did I want to be when I was growing up?* Always a football player. But I wanted more than that. I wanted a big life. A fun life. I wanted to live a rap video. Popping bottles, tossing hundreds at the strip club. Driving a Ferrari. Or even better, a jacked-up custom pickup truck. I wanted a girl who loved me. Who wanted to go on adventures with me.

I remember, years ago, seeing the viral video of Jennifer Edward's stripper fail. I loved that she was wild and crazy but that she seemed really grounded. She's changed though. I guess I have, too. Both of us morphed into different versions of ourselves because of our relationships. The crazy thing is, I didn't realize it was happening.

Last year, when Lori's family came for Christmas, her younger sister said that she was having trouble meeting a good man. She wondered why she couldn't find one like me.

Lori laughed haughtily and said, *Honey, they don't come this way. What you see took years of training.*

Now, I feel lost. Stuck between what I've become and what I once was.

I run the rest of my errands, go home, and get everything prepped.

I take the arrangement, removing the balloons, and sneak them over to Jennifer's room. Thankfully, she's not there. I use a scrap of paper from Jadyn's desk to make a card and write Jennifer a note.

I'M NOT SURE where Jennifer is, but I need to talk to Jadyn, so I give her a quick call. "Hey, you home?"

"Not yet. The Nebraska game is on soon, so I ran to the store to get some stuff for snacks. I just pulled into the subdivision."

"Is Jennifer with you?"

"No, she went to the spa with Devaney."

"How did that happen?" I ask in shock.

"Why don't I tell you when I get there?"

A few moments later, she's pulling into the driveway. Instead of going into the garage like usual, she turns off the engine and pops out.

"You leaving again?" I ask.

"No, Chase is turning the garage into his own private dance room."

"What for?"

"A lot has happened since you left this morning. Jennifer went over to your house to check on Dani. They apparently had a really good breakfast and a really good talk. While Jenn was cleaning up, Dani came over and apologized to Chase. They made up—thank goodness—and even though you told her she could still go to the dance, she decided not to. Chase and Damon were supposed to go to a birthday party tonight. Chase can't go because he is grounded, but he would have bailed anyway. He's creating a dance for Dani; he even bought her flowers."

I scratch my head. The thought of someone doing something like that for my baby makes me crazy. Because I know exactly *why* boys do romantic shit. The same reason my car is full of champagne and flowers.

"Would you rather she be with Dalton?" she asks, seeing my distress. "Two things: I saw his father at the grocery store. His throwing hand is broken, meaning he's out for the season. He didn't get grounded, but his date for the dance did, so Dalton asked Dani to go with him instead. That means, your daughter turned down going to the dance with arguably the most popular senior boy. And I'd be willing to bet that you can thank Jennifer for that. What are the balloons for?"

I swallow back the lump I feel in my throat and give my best friend a hug. "They are for you. I'm sorry I was a jerk this morning. You were completely right."

"Can you say that again? I'd like to record it," she says with an easy laugh.

"This is definitely an off-the-record apology," I say, laughing, too.

"So, are you taking her out in public?"

"Not until after Wednesday. Then I don't care what anyone thinks."

"Good for you," she says. "Wanna help me carry the groceries in?"

"I would, but I have to get home. Do me a favor. Make sure Jennifer goes up to her room before I come pick her up."

"Like, she's not just walking over to your house?"

"No, I'll be picking her up."

"Uh, okay," she says.

I load groceries into her arms and then go open the door for her.

"You'll see," I say.

Jennifer

"I'M SURPRISED YOU didn't invite Danny over to watch the game," I say to Jadyn, who is effortlessly throwing together a huge spread of food.

If I had this many people over all the time, I'd have a catering company on speed dial. But then I think of how wonderful it was to make breakfast for Dani this morning, and I realize that, to Jadyn, food is part of the way she shows her love for her friends and family.

"He knows he's always invited," she tells me. "He has other plans tonight. With you."

"Is it because he didn't want me to hang out with you all?"

"I think it's more that he doesn't want us all hanging out with you."

"What do you think I should wear?"

"Remember the dress I told you to keep covered up until you needed it? I think you need it."

"Oh gosh, the pressure. Is he taking me somewhere all fancy?"

"I'm not sure," she says noncommittally.

And I know she's not going to say anything more on the subject.

"Danny came over before he left for work this morning to invite me out for dinner tonight. After he left, I was being all girlie and watched him walk away. It seemed like you two had a disagreement."

"Yeah, well, Danny and I tend to butt heads sometimes on certain subjects."

"And am I one of those subjects?"

She drops the cheese on the counter and looks me directly in the eye. "Not at all. Obviously. Things are just complicated with him not yet being divorced."

"That makes sense," I say, still wondering what they disagreed about when a bunch of kids come barreling in from the garage.

"Mom, Jennifer, come see what we did!" Haley yells. "Maddie, Kassie, and I have been helping Chase all day!"

I get off the barstool while Jadyn wipes her hands on a towel.

The garage is completely transformed. There is black plastic sheeting hanging around the room, hiding the normal garage contents. Four disco lights dangle from the ceiling along with multiple strands of colored Christmas lights. There's a massive banner spelling out *Homecoming* in blue glitter. They even laid down carpet. And not just any carpet. This carpet appears to glow in the dark. Off to the side, there is a dining room table elaborately and colorfully set for two. I'm talking napkins, wine glasses, and a tablecloth made out of pink sequins. Angel, the dog, is decked out in a matching pink boa and doesn't seem to mind.

"Wow. This is something," Jadyn says. She wanders around the room, inspecting all their work and beaming with pride. "Devaney is going to love it. Good job. And, because it was so sweet of you girls to help Chase, why don't you call your parents and see if you can sleep over tonight?"

"Really, Mom?" Haley asks, running up and giving her mother a hug. "That's perfect. They can help me serve dinner. Did you get everything?"

"Of course I did," Jadyn says with a grin.

"It will be Dani's first time," Chase says proudly, causing my mind to immediately go to sex.

Are they really setting this all up so that he can have sex with Danny's daughter?

"Um, first time for *what*?" I blurt out, suddenly feeling very protective of her.

"Oh." Chase immediately blushes. "Our family has a tradition. When something good happens, we get a bucket of chicken, all the fixings, and a bottle of champagne to celebrate."

"The kids get sparkling cider," Jadyn clarifies.

"And Dani doesn't know about this? I thought you guys were all so close?" I ask.

The kids' eyes get that deer-in-the-headlights look.

"You guys did great," Jadyn says. "Chase, go get dressed. I picked up the wrist corsage, and it's in the fridge. Everything else is in the kitchen. Why don't you girls go put it on my good china?"

The kids and the dog all go running off.

"Did I say something wrong?" I ask.

"No, it's just that …" She sighs heavily. "How can I put this? Um, Lori pretty much didn't approve of anything that wasn't top notch. She thought fried chicken and champagne were the ultimate in tacky. And I know this because, when I told her it was kind of a thing with me and Phillip, she told me so. We never invited the Diamonds to celebrate with us in that way. I didn't want her to taint my children. I never wanted them thinking they were too good for a bucket of chicken. Sure, Phillip and I earn more money now, and the champagne we buy is a lot nicer quality than it used to be, but it's always got to be passed around and drunk straight from the bottle."

My heart swells in admiration. "If it wasn't for Danny, you wouldn't have stayed friends with Lori, would you?"

"Absolutely not. I always tell my kids to be careful when choosing their words because words can hurt as much as physical pain. That if you say something, even out of anger, if it's hurtful enough, the other person might never be able to forget it. That's where I've been with her since. I've forgiven her. I'm polite and friendly to her out of respect for Danny and the kids. Otherwise, I would have put her out of my life a very long time ago. Because life is too short."

"Here, here," I say, raising my empty hand in the air.

"We can't have that," she says, sneaking behind the black plastic and coming back with two bottles of beer. She clinks them together and says, "Here's to true friends." She takes a drink and glances at her watch. "What time is your date?"

"Fifteen minutes."

"You'd better go get ready!"

I give her a quick hug and then run out the side door and up the stairs. When I get to the door to my bedroom, I find a large vase wrapped in orange tissue paper and covered with silly

Halloween stickers, a note poking out from underneath it.

I carry it into the bedroom, set it on the dresser, and then peel off the tissue, being careful not to rip it. What I find is a crazy floral arrangement that makes my heart sing. There are about a million orange roses. Mixed in between is an assortment of sparkling, twisting neon-green sticks, glittered hot-pink skulls, shimmering black bats, and sugared orange pumpkins.

The result is both extravagant and completely tacky—much like the homecoming dance in the garage below me—yet it feels utterly romantic.

I rush into the bathroom, touch up my makeup, and then unzip the dress bag. The first thing I notice is that the dress is orange. I close my eyes, remembering the last time I wore an orange dress. It's always been my favorite color, and it looks pretty with my skin tone, but after I won an Academy Award and was labeled best dressed of the night, my stylist said we had to retire the color in honor.

Part of me wants to start crying. The other part wants to see the rest of this dress. I pull it all the way out of the bag and discover a ruffled mini made of silk satin. It feels so soft against my skin, and when I catch a glimpse of myself in the mirror, I let out a little squeal and then jump up and down. Imagine a basic, fitted V-neck shift and sew some ruffles around the hem. Add more ruffles to drape across your shoulders and arms, and you have the amazingness of this adorable dress. It's both sexy and casual.

I don't know where Danny is taking me tonight, but it doesn't matter. I feel beautiful.

I noticed there was a shoebox nestled in the bottom of the dress bag, so I get it out. I let out a laugh when I find a pair of strappy hot-pink suede sandals and a Bordeaux-colored mini handbag. I'm still laughing as I finish getting dressed. I look a little like my flowers.

I quickly put the shoes on and run into the bathroom to add a bright lip color. I realize I've yet to read the note. I rush over and pick it up, just as there's a knock on the door.

You make me feel young and reckless.

—Danny

There's another knock.

I take a moment to savor the sentiment before I open the door.

"Wow. You look … freaking gorgeous," Danny says breathlessly.

"Thank you," I say with a smile. "Plus, my dress sort of matches the flowers you sent. They are crazy beautiful."

"You're crazy beautiful," he says. "The flowers are just plain crazy. Do you like them?"

"Like them? Are you kidding? I love them. They are so fun. And silly. But then there are all those roses. They smell amazing. Thank you."

Danny beams and holds his arm out. "Sorry I'm a little late. I had to take some pictures of Devaney in her homecoming dress. You ready to go?"

"I am." I take a few steps out into the office.

He falls in step next to me, putting his hand on the small of my back.

"Danny, you're killing me with that."

His hand stays put. Clearly, he doesn't have a clue.

"With what?" he asks, looking perplexed.

I slightly lean back and then pull my hips forward, curving my spine away from his hand.

"My hand? Is that inappropriate?" he asks, finally understanding. "I was just trying to be polite."

"So, you do that to every woman you walk next to? Because I'm going to have a problem with that."

"Am I in trouble?" he asks, genuinely looking upset.

The change in his demeanor says everything—that his wife flew off the handle about stuff like this. That he's used to being scolded.

I take a step toward him, bringing the whole front of my body flat against his, and then wrap my arms around his neck.

"When I press against you like this"—I squirm a little for effect—"does it feel polite?" He shakes his head, so I keep going, "What you might not know, Danny Diamond, is, it doesn't matter where you touch me; it feels like magic. Your fingers have a power over me. Anytime we are close, my heart beats a little faster, but when you throw in a touch, your adorable smirk, your commercial-worthy voice"—I press my nose to his neck—"and the way you smell, it's like you're imprinting a part of you onto me. Every time you do it, I feel elation, quickly followed by an intense flash of sorrow."

"It makes you sad when I touch you?"

"It makes me remember that you might decide *not* to keep touching me. When we met, you were married, and you purposely didn't touch me."

"I couldn't. It would have—" he argues.

"I know, but what you don't realize is that you did touch me. And, believe me, I felt every single accidental brush. When we walked into the restaurant so long ago, you touched the small of my back. Like you did just now. Maybe I didn't have the same impact on you as you had on me, but—"

"That's not true," he states adamantly. "I was a wreck for weeks, trying to decide what to do. I felt like my life had finally gotten started. I had the career of my dreams, I was married, and I had a baby. I came home, wanting to blow it all up, run back to California, and be with you. After you dropped me off at the airport, I sat there and wondered what in the world I was doing. I didn't want to go home at all. But then I convinced myself that I was starstruck. That it was all ego. Like, *Look at me now; I can pull a chick of this caliber because I'm a professional quarterback.*"

"But you knew better once you stopped freaking out. That's why you stopped talking to me."

"Because I knew it was more. That, in one night, I had fallen in love with you. But I was too afraid to act on it. I was afraid of what would happen if I blew up my life."

"Afraid you'd lose your daughter," I say knowingly. "Jadyn told me that your wife threatened you."

He hangs his head. I kiss his nose in response, causing him to look up into my eyes.

"I don't want to talk anymore about what could have been back then," I tell him. "I was just letting you know that, every time you touch me, I feel like we have a future, and if that's not what you want, save me the heartache. Don't do it."

He nods, grins at me, and then puts his hand back where it was, causing me to smile so big, it almost hurts my face. We go down the stairs and follow the path to where a shiny red Ferrari convertible is sitting in the drive.

Danny

"OH MY GOSH, Danny. This car is beautiful. It's a F430 Spider, right?" Jennifer asks, causing my face to light up over the fact that she knows.

"That's right."

"You must hardly ever drive it. If that's the case," she says with a smirk, "then you should let me drive it to dinner."

"I don't drive it as much as I'd like. To be honest, Lori hates this car. It wasn't even allowed in the garage. Although that's not a bad thing since the kids were always in and out of it with their bikes and sports gear when they were younger."

"Yeah, you wouldn't want this scratched up," she says, delicately running her hand across the hood as she circles the car to look at it from all angles.

"Do you like cars?" I ask.

"I have a thing for exotic cars. When I first started acting, I made a lot of money doing the Sector movies. So, for fun, my friends and I made a list of the most ridiculously expensive cars. I didn't want to buy one until I saw the Bentley Continental GT3-R. They were really rare at the time. So, the party where I met you, it was a fundraiser for Moon Wish Wine, remember?"

"I remember everything about the night," I say, just watching her walk the perimeter of my car, taking in every curve.

"I was dating the actor, Knox Daniels, at the time."

"I definitely remember that. Jadyn was shocked that I could steal you away from the Sexiest Man Alive."

She giggles. "Well, he is pretty cute, I'll say that. So if you saw every movie I was in, does that mean you saw all the *Daddy's Angel* movies?"

"Oh, yeah. You played a very naughty girl in that series. It was hot."

"The producer of that series was Riley Johnson. He had a GT3-R and let me drive it. Since then, I've been a little obsessed. I have a storage unit with, um, six-ish cars." She rolls her eyes and lets out a howling laugh. "By *six-ish*, I mean, there are nine. I made a bet with Riley that, if *Daddy's Angels* hit big, he'd sell me the car. I won. It was the start of my collection."

She moves to the driver's side, opens the door, and slides in.

"Did I say you could drive?"

"Nope. I figure it's better to ask for forgiveness later," she teases, leaning toward me as I slip into the passenger seat next to her.

I'd let her drive anything of mine she wants.

She turns the key and revs the engine, grinning like a maniac at the throaty sound. "Ohmigawd! This is going to be so fun. I hope we are going on the highway."

"We are now," I tell her as she backs out of the driveway.

She takes off in the direction I point. Today was sunny and warm, but the temperature cooled when the sun set. Jennifer doesn't seem to even notice. Her hair is blowing in the breeze. The ruffles on her dress are rippling across her skin. And the grin on her freaking gorgeous face brings me such joy.

She babbles on about the different cars she has, how I will have to come to California to see and drive them, and how responsive the throttle on my car is. Based on her knowledge of cars, I'm thinking she's not just bullshitting me. I will admit, I am kinda thinking about how responsive *my* throttle feels whenever she's around.

I direct her out of our subdivision and onto the freeway. Thankfully, it's not too busy because she was serious when she said she liked to drive fast. We've gone about six miles before I suggest she take the next exit. I take her a different way, but we're soon turning back into my neighborhood.

"Wait," she says, "isn't this where you live?"

"Yeah," I say, pointing out a couple of more turns. I take the remote out of my pocket and click it, causing the garage door to roll up.

"I thought we were going out? I got dressed up," she says, looking slightly stricken.

"And you're wearing orange. Are you cheering for the other team?" I tease.

"Oh, so we are going to the Mackenzies' to watch the game?" she asks.

I take her hand and help her out of the car, and then I lead her in through the front door.

"I can't believe I'm about to say this, but I guess there's a first time for everything." I show her the dining room, where the table is set for dinner and dozens of votive candles flicker softly. "There are some things more important than a Nebraska game."

Her eyes light up, the candles reflecting in them. She wraps an arm around my neck and pulls me close. "It's beautiful, Danny."

I give her a quick kiss on the cheek and then slide a chair out for her. "Please, have a seat."

"Did you cook?"

"No. I wanted to take you to my favorite restaurant, but Jadyn thought it would be a bad idea. If we were seen together, not only would the press know you were here, but they might also speculate things about us. And those things would be bad for me."

"Like, because of your endorsements?"

"No one knows that I'm getting a divorce. So, it would have looked a little scandalous."

She shimmies her shoulders and grins. "I'm feeling a little scandalous. Between the crazy, gorgeous flowers and that exhilarating drive, who knows what I might do? Speaking of that, your car only has, like, five thousand miles on it. What's up with that? Did you purposely try to keep the milage low? I figured with the way your wife seemed to be into status, it would have gotten driven a lot more."

"I bought the car with my sign-on bonus when I got drafted. I also bought it when I was a little drunk during Phillip's bachelor party in Vegas. She always considered my money as *our* money, and it pissed her off that I hadn't gotten her approval first. She also didn't like that I refused to return the car, even after she went nearly ballistic."

I pour the wine and bring our meal out from the kitchen.

"I'm getting the hang of this," Jennifer says, raising her glass into the air, "and I like it. If it's okay with you, I'd like to do the toast."

I give her a nod.

"To being reckless," she says, looking straight into my eyes, almost daring me to be exactly that.

Jennifer

WE'VE TALKED ALL the way through dinner. Although I really just want to strip naked and do it on the table, I'm enjoying getting to know him and understanding his life better.

"The ribs were amazing, and the cheesy corn is literally to die for. I sort of want to bathe in it."

Danny grins.

I love how easy it is to make him smile. And I find myself wanting to do it. But I realize that it's not my job to make him happy. He's either happy with his life and with me in it or he's not. I have to fight every urge I have to kiss it and make it better, because I know, based on my experience with Troy, it doesn't work.

I will admit though, part of me wants him to kiss me to fix the shambles that my life has become. I also know I can't hide out here forever. Pretty soon, I'm going to have to go back to LA. Find somewhere to live. Meet with my agent, assistant, and publicist to figure out what I am contractually bound to do. I know there isn't too much as I had planned on taking some time off during Troy's upcoming tour.

"Jadyn told me you came over and spoke with Devaney and went to the spa with her today. I just want you to know, I appreciate that. And it sounds like you gave her some good advice."

"Ha!" I say with a laugh. "I told her, once an asshole, always an asshole. She decided on her own which category that quarterback fit into. I know last night was rough, but you should be proud of her. She's a good kid."

"I have two amazing children, but I can tell high school is going to be tough."

"I was best friends with a girl who had the coolest family. They did so much together, and they had fun. Everyone wanted to be around them. Me especially. I didn't get along with my mom, and I certainly never confided in her about anything. My friend told her mom almost everything. Anything she didn't tell her, we did. I always wanted that kind of family." I set my napkin on the table. "So, Danny Diamond, dinner is finished. What do you have planned next for our date?"

"Um," he stutters.

I realize I'm an idiot. *Why does my mouth not filter for my brain?*

"I don't mean that I expect anything else. I mean, the flowers, the drive, the dinner, all the candles. It was really special, Danny. I was just going to suggest something, but I didn't want to if you had something else in mind."

"What were you thinking?" he asks.

"Well, what would you be doing tonight if I wasn't here? Like, it's a normal night in your life."

"I'd be watching the game next door. Or, if the game was already over, I'd be watching film in my study."

"Film? Like a movie?" I ask.

"No, like game film of the opponents we'll be facing next."

I clap. "Oh, then that's what I want to do!"

"Really?" he asks, causing me to realize I should have suggested something that included us naked.

He blows out the candles and then leads me into his study. He sits in one of the oversize chairs. I could sit in the matching chair, but I decide not to. Instead, I plop down sideways across his lap with the rest of the second bottle of wine.

He grabs a remote, turning on both the TV and fireplace. I sort of thought that we would be watching a game, but this is like snippets of plays. A football montage.

"What are we looking for?" I ask. "Like, that was a good play by the defense. They stopped the run."

"Right," he says. "The hole closed before he could penetrate it."

"That sounds dirty!" I slap his knee and bust out in laughter.

"Watch this," he says, scrolling through to another play. "In this one, he got penetration in the backfield."

"Ohmigawd! Did he enjoy it at least?"

Danny laughs along with me. "Probably not. He got tackled pretty hard. See this defensive back? He's the best player on the team, and I'll be his prime target. See how unstoppable he is? How he got right through the offensive line?"

"He came from his blindside and got him from behind," I say after watching the quarterback take a vicious sack.

Danny raises his eyebrows at me.

"Oh, I just did it, too, and didn't even notice! What happens when *you* get it from behind, Danny?"

He stares at me, not sure of what to say, but the corners of his mouth are curled up into a smirk. "I'm trying to think of something fun and sexual to say to make you laugh, but I'm coming up blank. I'll tell you my favorite one though."

"What is it?" I ask, leaning closer to him. So close, our lips almost touch when we speak. "He. Could. Go. All. The. Way."

"Quarterbacks like going all the way, huh?" I flirt, sliding my hand behind his neck and giving him a kiss.

We kiss for a few minutes. Even though I'm a little tipsy, either from being this close to Danny or the wine, I don't try to move things along. I'm okay with just kissing him.

God, how long has it been since I just made out with someone?

"After that kiss," he says, "I might need to go to the sideline for a quick blow."

My eyes get big, but then … "Wait, *sideline for a quick blow* probably doesn't mean what my dirty mind is thinking."

He chuckles and allows his fingers to graze down my arm as he answers, "When someone runs hard down the field, they'll come over and get some oxygen to help their muscles recover quicker."

"That's funny. Oh! Rewind that! Listen to what the announcer just said."

He hits rewind, and we watch as the chains are brought out to see if it was a first down or not. It's just short.

The announcer goes, "Well, football is a game of inches."

"Oh, you have a dirty mind," Danny says. "I have never taken it that way before, now it's all I'll think about every time I hear it said."

"And how many inches do *you* have?" I shimmy my butt against his lap.

He grabs my hips. And his hands, I realize, are quite large. They splay all the way across my stomach.

"You'd better behave."

Of course, I am not the kind of girl who behaves, so I press my ass into his lap again and wiggle it.

"Now, you're in trouble," he says, tickling my sides.

When I scream out in laughter, he shuts me up with more kisses.

Can I just say that I love the way Danny kisses? Or maybe it's the way we kiss. You know how, sometimes, you kiss someone, and it just feels sort of off. Like, your tongues collide rather than move in synchrony. Our kissing is *not* like that. It's a perfect dance, a rhythm only we can feel. His lips are soft, his tongue firm and demanding, and then there's the scruff of his facial hair. It's like perfection. If our relationship were based solely on the way his kisses make me feel, I would live out the rest of my days in a visceral bliss.

The TV blares back on; apparently, it got tired of being on pause while we made out.

"That's loud," Danny mutters, barely moving his lips away from mine. He grabs the remote and presses pause again.

"I'm enjoying kissing you," I tell him as I take the remote and hit play. "But I'm enjoying the football part, too."

We watch a few more plays, and then Danny points at the screen. "Watch this. The quarterback is going deep. That's where the defense is vulnerable and something I hope to capitalize on during the game on Monday."

I grin at him. "He's going *deep*, huh?"

He rolls his eyes. "Dang, now everything I say is going to be sexual. Especially when you see the next play. They are close to the goal line, and all they have to do is *pound it in*."

I let out a hoot of laughter. He tickles me. I hop off his lap and stand in front of him.

I blow a pretend whistle and signal a penalty. "Illegal use of the hands," I say, pointing to my sides where he keeps tickling me before dropping back down across his lap.

He just sits there and looks at me, causing me to worry that something is on my face.

"What?" I finally ask.

"I've never done anything like this before," he says. "It's really fun."

"Your wife never watched films with you?"

He vehemently shakes his head. "She didn't like football, and I think, half the time, she thought watching films was just an excuse for me to be alone. I tried to teach her. In college, when we dated, she was interested, but she got bored with it, I guess."

"That makes me sad for you. It's so obvious how much you love the game."

"Were you bored?" he asks, looking concerned.

"Me? Are you kidding? I was sitting on your lap, Danny Diamond. You could have been watching a math video, and I would have enjoyed it. You allowed me into your world. You taught me a lot of dirty football terms that I believe will be useful in my life and—" I stop mid-sentence to stare at him. "Gosh, I've missed you." I shake my head and ramble, "That makes no sense, does it? One night, one kiss on the lips, a football game, a hayrack ride."

"I kissed the back of your hand when we said good-bye. Can't forget that." He slides his finger to the spot.

"And I autographed your arm."

"I didn't wash it for days." He stretches his long arm over to his desk, opens a drawer, fishes around, and then produces a black Sharpie. I smile, unbutton his shirtsleeve, and slowly roll it up. His eyes are hooded and sexy as the tip of the marker touches his skin. Writing on him feels almost sensual.

I sign my name, adding a heart to the top of the *I*, just like I did back then. I also have a strong desire to see more of him unclothed.

"I've seen your underwear ads, and I know you have tattoos. Can I see them?" I ask, figuring that's one easy way to get him out of his shirt. *And is it bad that I'm hoping he has a few tats hiding under his pants?*

He doesn't reply, just starts unbuttoning his shirt, and then moves me over, so he can stand. My heart races. I hear a creak coming from somewhere in the house. *The wind maybe? Or his kids?* Part of me wants to tell him to put the shirt back on, so we don't get caught, but the other part of me wants him to take all his clothes off. *Probably just the wind. Please be just the wind.*

When his dress shirt slides off his shoulders, instead of seeing the spectacular pecs and abs I've seen in magazines, I realize he's wearing a T-shirt underneath.

Don't get me wrong; it's a nice view. Tightly molded to his

chest, it's like a movie-trailer teaser with a glimpse of what's to come.

I'm hoping our movie is one full of beautiful sexual expression. And dare I wish for love? An over-the-top proposal, a romantic happy ending, driving-off-in-the-sunset happily ever after. You'd think, with all the movies I'd made, I'd have thought about my own life with Troy as one. A chance encounter at a wedding, moving in together shortly after, and traveling the world is the stuff fairy tales are made of. Except alcohol was the evil stepmother in our story, undermining us at every turn, causing me to lose myself while trying to save him.

"This one," Danny says, bringing me back to the present, pointing at tall Roman numerals on the inside of his forearm, opposite of where I wrote my name, "are the dates of my children's births."

I slide my finger across the top of the tattoo. "That's sweet."

"It's off center," he says with a sigh. "I started it close to my elbow so that I'd have room for *all* my children's birthdays."

I look at the now sad-looking empty space between the middle of his forearm and wrist. "You wanted more kids?"

He nods. "Yeah. I'm an only child, and I've always dreamed of having a big family. Lots of kids and grandkids."

"How come you didn't have more?"

"Once we got a boy and a girl, Lori said we were done. Our perfect family was complete. She hated being pregnant."

"I've always wanted children," I whisper, thinking I'd like to help him fill in the empty space.

"Why didn't you?"

"My dad was an alcoholic. I swore, I'd never bring a child into a situation like that. I remember a few years after being with Troy, I was so excited because I was a few days late. I was thinking of how I was going to get a pregnancy test the next day and how happy I would be if I were pregnant. That night was when Troy had his first relapse. It was ugly and hurtful, but I understood the addiction even though I didn't get it. Like, I don't know how you could be so weak as to let something rule your life. Now, I realize I did that, too. I allowed Troy and his addiction to rule my life, which is almost as bad."

"Have you talked to him since it happened? Where do things stand with the two of you? Will you get a divorce?"

"We were together for a long time but never got married. So, after all that happened last weekend, I was hiding out in the house, trying to wrap my head around it. Trying to mourn what I knew was the end of our relationship. Then, he and his manager just walked in the front door on Wednesday afternoon with no warning. He was all, *Sorry*, and, *Don't leave me*. Thank goodness Jadyn had texted just before, or I don't know where I would've gone. Over the years I had been with Troy, although his popularity grew worldwide and his music was golden, we lost a lot of friends. Well, I did. Party friends are surprisingly easy to find. It's easy to get caught up in the lifestyle."

Danny slips his arm around my shoulders and hugs me. "I'm sorry you had to go through that."

"I'm sorry you are going through a divorce."

"Thank you."

We have a quiet moment of just looking at each other, our hearts speaking volumes but our words stuck in our throats.

I expect for him to kiss me, but instead, he says, "Want to see the rest?"

And I'm thinking, *The rest of what?*

I then remember asking to see his tattoos.

He pulls his T-shirt up on one side, and I can't contain my gasp.

"I know I shouldn't so blatantly drool over your muscles. We all know things like a fit body and good looks fade over the years, and it's important to love the person's insides and their being, but, damn, Danny, is all of your body perfection?"

He stops and gives me a cocky grin. "Wanna find out?"

But then he stops and backs away. Shakes his head. "I'm sorry. That was completely inappropriate of me."

"Why?"

"It's late," he says, glancing at his watch. "I'd better get to bed."

Wait, is he inviting me to join him? Can I stand up, kick my feet together with a, Yee-haw, *and break out in song?*

I glance at his bedroom door.

His eyes follow mine, and then a sad look crosses his face as he takes my hand and says, "I'll walk you out."

He's kicking me out?

"Okay," I say, suddenly upset.

When he opens the door, I step outside and don't bother to look back. "Night," is all I mutter.

He shuts the door behind me. I stand there for a few minutes, wondering what just happened before dropping down on the front stoop to cry.

Danny

I CLOSE THE door, feeling like I just shut my heart in it. I peek out the dining room window, making sure Jennifer can't see me as she walks next door. But she's not there.

I have a moment of panic. *Where did she go?* I stand directly in front of the window, not caring now if she sees me, and look down both sides of the street. She's nowhere.

I run to the front door and open it, finding her sitting on the top step, her head bowed toward her knees, crying.

Shit.

I gently shut the door and sit down next to her. "Why are you crying?"

She shakes her head. "I'm not sure. All of it, I guess."

"All of *it*, or all of *me*?"

She looks up, tears streaming down her face. "You."

"I should have had the courtesy to walk you home. I know that. But, if I had …"

"What?"

"I would have kissed you good night. And, I wouldn't have stopped there."

"I wouldn't have wanted you to."

"My kids could come home any minute."

"So, you and your wife never had sex? No wonder she looked elsewhere," she says, her comment stinging. "Night, Danny. Good luck with your game. I'm going to head back to LA on Monday. Get my life together, and stop hiding out here, in the middle of nowhere."

Her chin is jutted out. The hurt I've caused is written all across her face.

I reach out and take her hand, pulling her up. I lead her across the yard and then up the stairs to Jadyn's office.

I follow her into the room.

When the door closes, it's dark, just a little moonlight coming in through the window.

"Jennifer, it's taken me months to come to terms with the fact that my marriage is over. I'm rebuilding my life, my kids' lives, and I'm trying to figure out a settlement with Lori. I'm a few days away from knowing when it will be over, when I can start over. If she signs the papers on Wednesday, it will be thirty days. You just ended your long relationship a week ago.

"I can't kiss you again because, if I do, I'll end up in bed with you or probably on this table and everywhere else we can think of.

I'm ready for that, but I don't think you are. I know you say you're done with him, but I can't … let myself be with you like that when I don't know. Maybe Jadyn's right, and I am being a pussy, but I finally get now why she was afraid to date Phillip after they were friends for so long. She was afraid it wouldn't work, and she'd lose him. I lost you once by my own doing, and I don't have the strength right now to lose you again."

I bring her hand to my lips, pressing it into my skin, just like I did at the end of our night together all those years ago.

I pull my hand away, and she throws herself into my arms.

"Jadyn suggested that I hang out with you, be friends. Can we do that? Do you want to get to know each other better? Take it slow?" I ask. Well, beg really.

"Yes," she says, "but I need you to know that I'm not going to get back together with Troy this time. I shouldn't have taken him back after the second rehab, and I told him I wouldn't if there were a third. I can't be with him, Danny. I don't want to be. I don't know if we will work, and I don't want you to think this is me rebounding. I told you that night, and I'll tell you again. If you can't promise forever, just promise tonight."

I lower my lips to hers, giving her only a taste.

Then, I walk away.

As I close the door behind me, I turn around. "I want forever more than I want tonight, Jennifer. If you go back to LA on Monday, I hope you know that it was really nice seeing you again."

OCTOBER 29TH

Danny

"IS JENNIFER NOT coming to the party?" Phillip asks me.

"I don't think so. She said something last night about going home tomorrow."

I don't tell him how our night ended, but he must be able to tell from the look on my face.

"Do you want to talk about it?" he asks.

"Last night was really fun. We watched game film after dinner. She sat on my lap. She enjoyed being with me and doing something I loved. Remember in high school how you'd invite a girl over, but you'd end up kissing through most of the movie?"

"Yeah. Heck, Jadyn and I rarely see the movie still. Or we have to rewind a lot."

"It started like that. That fun, flirty beginning of a relationship. The problem is, every time I feel like I want to take things further, I stop myself."

"Why?"

"Why do you think?" I throw my hands into the air. "She's going back to LA. This was a convenient place for her to hide out. That's it. Even though she says she can see a future with us together, she's freaking leaving, which says it all."

"Danny, it's not like she can't come back."

"And what about the kids? And, no, I'm not using them as an

excuse. It's a legitimate concern. I can't move to LA or fly off to see her. I have responsibilities here. Although I think the beach is gorgeous, I'm a Midwestern boy. I like the seasons. I like the people. It's home. I won't uproot my kids. And I'm technically still married. Regardless of my wife's morals, I don't want the kids to think it's okay. Because, to me, it's not. I can't handle the thought of Jennifer leaving tomorrow, but I have to let her go. LA is her home. And you need to make sure Jadyn lets her go, too."

"Better watch what you say next," Phillip says. "She's coming this way."

Jadyn bounds up to us and grabs Phillip's tie. He's dressed as Clark Kent—long-sleeved shirt and loosened tie, dress pants and suspenders, hair slicked back, and black glasses. His shirt is unbuttoned to reveal a shiny red Superman shirt. Jadyn is Lois Lane in a tight pencil skirt and business jacket. The rest of the family is dressed as different superheroes. Chase is Spider-Man, Haley is Wonder Woman, Ryder is Batman, Madden is the Flash, and the dog is Captain America.

"I think we're going to win the contest this year," she says to Phillip. "Danny, I'm surprised you didn't dress up."

Joey, one of my high school friends and his youngest son join us. Their family—which includes wife, Chelsea; daughter, Jaci; and sons, Jack and Jacob—are dressed as zombies with elaborate face paint.

"What's that say?" Jack asks Jadyn, pointing to the steno notebook in her hand.

She flips it up, and Jacob reads, "*I beat Superman.* No way, Superman is unbeatable," he says and then takes off when he sees Ryder.

"Not if you know how to do it right," Jadyn quips.

This causes Joey to hoot with laughter, and Phillip gives Jadyn a sexy smirk, followed by a kiss. She flips the other side over and shows it to us.

I'm his kryptonite.

"Now, that is a freaking true statement if there ever were one." Joey laughs again.

I glance up, movement from a window above the garage catching my attention. I pretend to look straight at Jadyn but use my peripheral vision to see Jennifer sitting in the window seat, looking down at us. Although I can't see her face, I know she's feeling left out.

I took Dani and Damon to get their costumes a few weeks ago. Dani is a sparkling unicorn, and Damon is a skeleton. I overheard him tell Chase that he was going to let girls know they were free to *jump his bones.* Kid's a chip off the old block.

I look down at myself and then at my friends and their families, who, unlike me, are all dressed up and having fun. Halloween has always been my favorite holiday. Lori took that away from me, too, I realize.

I glance back up at the window.

"Jadyn, do you still have those costumes from last year? The ones you didn't wear?"

"Yeah."

"Could I borrow them?"

"Sure, come with me," she says with a grin.

She leads me into their basement storage room, scanning the plastic totes. "What happened with you and Jennifer last night? She hasn't left her room today. And I overheard you tell Phillip that she's going back home tomorrow."

I run my hand through my hair. "You told me I had to be careful until Wednesday."

"In public. No one knows what happens behind closed doors, Danny."

"I made her cry," I admit. "Look, I'm going to try to make it up to her. Just find the costumes, okay?"

She pulls the costumes out. "Since they are all wrapped in

plastic, they aren't wrinkled. You should be good to go."

"Thanks."

I go into the guest bath and put on my costume, slip out into the garage, and then run up the stairs to Jennifer's room.

Jennifer

I WAKE UP late, wrap myself up in the fluffy robe that was hanging in the bathroom, make myself a cup of coffee from the machine in Jadyn's office, and then sit sideways on the window seat, looking down at the Mackenzies' backyard. The Halloween party has started. Phillip is helping kids into a bounce house, Chase is attaching a skull-shaped piñata under the large black spider on top of the monkey bars, Nick is helping an adorable little girl bob for apples, and Dani is handing out caramel apples to everyone. It's like a scene out of a freaking Rockwell painting.

Tears fall down my face as I wish that I were part of it. That a scene like this could be part of my reality. But it's not.

Danny was right for stopping things. It's only been a week since everything happened with Troy. It's only been a few days since I left town. And, for some stupid reason, I still feel responsible for Troy. I feel bad that I'm not there to help get him to rehab. I also feel bad that I told Danny I was going back to LA when it's the last thing I want to do. I'm not ready to face reality.

But I have to.

I didn't sleep last night. My words kept echoing in my head.

"If you can't promise forever, just promise tonight."

Back, when I'd first said it, I was being my flirty, bold self. It was cute. Last night, it made me sound desperate. That I'm willing to settle for one night with Danny when it's really not what I want.

Add to that the fact that Troy's texts have grown more desperate-sounding, and I made the mistake of answering the phone when he called at three in the morning.

Drunk.

I'm deep in thought, trying to figure out how I'm going to talk Troy into going back to rehab before he completely destroys everything he's worked so hard for, when a knock on the door startles me, almost causing me to spill my coffee.

I set the cup down, tighten up the robe, and open the door.

"Oh my gosh, Danny! What the heck are you wearing?" I laugh.

"I'm a rhinestone cowboy," he says.

"You have to come inside, so I can see that a little closer." When he does, I make him spin. "This might be the best costume I've ever seen. You know, with a name like Danny Diamond, you totally could have been a Vegas lounge singer. And this suit. Sparkling hot-pink leather, appliquéd with a green cactus, yellow mountains, and white clouds. And don't get me started on all the bling."

"I'm glad you like it. I was hoping you'd come to the party."

"Oh, I would, but I don't have a costume, so …" I lie. That's not why I'm not going.

He goes back outside, comes in, and says, "Thing is, I need a cowgirl." He holds up a very skimpy-looking black fringe and hot-pink costume. "Come on. It will be fun. I know you like candy." He starts to hand me the costume but then pulls it back. "I don't want you to feel obligated. It's just … I saw you in the window."

"When I saw you down there a few minutes ago, you weren't in a costume."

"I haven't dressed up for Halloween in years even though it was always my favorite holiday as a kid. For the most part, Lori found it tacky. If we did get invited to a more formal party, she would rent us elaborate costumes that usually smelled like mothballs." He takes me in his arms. "There's no one I'd rather dress up with than you."

"And where did you get these costumes on such short notice?"

"Jadyn bought them last year. Phillip wouldn't wear his because the pants were way too short. They were nonrefundable, so Jadyn kept them. It's kind of funny because, as soon as I saw the costume, I thought it looked like something I would wear, not Phillip."

"And, now, you are," I say compassionately. I grab the bag from his hand. "Stay here. I'll go put this on."

When I come back out, his mouth literally drops open. "You look … incredible. *Damn.*"

"You don't think it's a little too risqué for a backyard party?" I ask, looking down at the black lace one-piece topped with a black fringe skirt. A hot-pink suede belt wrapped low on my hips and a matching vest are the only things keeping it from being completely indecent.

"I think it's perfect for any party," he says, his eyes still blazing trails up and down my body.

"What about the boots?"

"I think the black suede thigh-highs are hot. Now that I've seen you in them, you can't wear anything else. This rhinestone cowboy is going to have rocks in his pants all night," he jokes.

"How about this?" I ask, putting on the pink suede cowboy hat.

"Gotta wear the hat," he says, pulling me back into his arms.

"We should take a picture!" I hold my phone out in front of us. When I snap it, he kisses the side of my face, giving me a goofy grin. "Ohmigawd, Danny, we're so cute!"

But it's so much more than that. They say a picture speaks a thousand words, and this one is saying that we both look incredibly happy.

"Come on, little doggie," he says, giving my butt a playful slap. "Let's get down there."

WE HAVE A ball at the party. There's music playing, face-painting, silly games, and lots of food and drink. Danny even clears out the bounce house, so the two of us can bounce around together. He told me that my skirt would be indecent while bouncing but that he didn't mind.

Just when I start thinking about the fun we could have tonight, he says, "I'm glad we dressed up, Jennifer. Thanks for coming to the party with me."

"Uh, are you leaving?"

"Yeah, I have to get to the hotel. The team stays together the night before each game."

"But I thought your game was here."

"We do it for both home and away games. It keeps players from partying the night before. We eat together and have team meetings to discuss the game plan. We even have a mandatory curfew."

"Oh," I say, feeling disappointed.

"Um, so I guess this is good-bye," he says, taking my hand and bringing it to his lips. "It was really nice seeing you, Jennifer. Have a great flight tomorrow."

And then he's gone without so much as a kiss.

OCTOBER 30TH

Jennifer

I'M AWOKEN BY the sound of knocking. I toss the fluffy comforter back and say, "Yes?" as I pull on a robe.

"It's Chase. Mom said to tell you there are warm cinnamon rolls on the counter, and if you want one, you should come get them. 'Cause my mom makes them from scratch. And they are really good. Okay, uh, bye. It was nice to meet you."

I hear footsteps across the wood floor, the door slamming shut, and then car doors and the garage door opening and closing.

Now that I'm awake, I notice the enticing smell of cinnamon. I go into the bathroom, run a brush through my hair before pulling it back in a ponytail, and decide to brush my teeth after I eat. I look at the clothes Jadyn bought me, all lined up in the closet, suddenly feeling like doing something I haven't in a long time—running. I work out with my trainer, have to in order to keep my figure camera ready, but at some point, I stopped running.

I thought it was because I had grown out of the need. Running was always my escape when I was young. When I started acting, it became my escape from the pressure—something I did just for me. When Troy suggested we share a trainer, even though Troy didn't work out often, I stopped running in favor of that.

I put on workout pants and a matching jacket and tie up the

running shoes.

However, I think I need to stop in the kitchen first.

When I swing the door to the office open, I notice a plain white envelope on the floor. I open it and pull out a ticket to tonight's game, a sideline pass, and a little note that says, *In case you decide to stay.* There's a heart and Danny's signature.

I clutch the ticket to my chest, emotions flooding me. I feel bad for making him think I was leaving. I thought if he thought I was leaving it might spur him on.

But Danny hasn't been behaving like most guys would in this situation. He hasn't been throwing himself at me. If anything, I feel like I've been the one pursuing him.

I make my way to the kitchen. Find a note from Jadyn, saying she has appointments most of the day but that it was really nice to see me. There's a phone number for a car service I can use to get to the airport.

I let out a whoosh of air, feeling like the wind got knocked out of me. She didn't say good-bye.

But then again, she opened her home when I needed it, and I didn't have the decency to tell her I was leaving. I'm a shitty friend.

I cover up the rolls, deciding to have one when I get back, do a few stretches, and then take off for my run. I have no idea where I'm going or if I'll ever be able to find my way back, but it feels good to be out here. My feet hit the pavement with a rhythmic sound, my breathing increases as my heart rate rises, and my mind clears.

I follow the road to a park that leads down to the lake. I head toward it and soon find myself sitting on a dock, cross-legged, looking out at the water.

It's a gorgeous late fall day. The air is a little crisp, but the sun is warm. A light breeze from the north causes gentle ripples to roll across the lake. I close my eyes and try to focus on my breathing.

When I open my eyes a short time later, I know what I need to do.

"YOU'RE STILL HERE," Dani says, coming through the Mackenzies' front door after school to find me camped out in my spot in the study. "Chase and Damon not home yet?"

"No, just me." I point down at the dog, who's been by my side all day, like she knew I needed the support. "And Angel."

"Angel seems to really like you," Dani says, causing the dog to furiously wag her tail.

"She's a good dog."

"She's a freak of nature," Dani says. "Most Labs don't live to be so old. Jadyn says it's because of all the love she gets here. She loves Chase the most though. Slept under his crib when he was a baby."

"I love her," I say, leaning down and letting the dog kiss my face. It's funny how good a dog can make you feel. Like you're not alone in the world. Like someone loves you. Besides having kids, a dog was always on my list of things I wanted in life. Maybe, someday, I'll buy a house with a big yard for a dog just like Angel. "I even love her name."

"Do you know how she got her name?" Dani asks.

"Because she's such a good dog?"

"No, when Jadyn was a senior in high school, her parents died in a car accident. A divorce is bad enough; I can't even imagine what it would be like to lose your parents so young. Her dad always called Jadyn his angel."

I let out a totally inappropriate snicker.

"I know, right?" she says. "If you've ever heard the stories about her and my dad when they were younger, I'm pretty sure she had her dad fooled. When Jadyn and Phillip were engaged and bought this house, my grandpa bought her Angel. The story goes that, on what was her dad's birthday, Grandpa went to a place where he and Jadyn's dad used to shoot skeet. They had a litter of puppies, and when the owner told them one was named Angel, he felt like it was a sign and brought her home."

"I'm surprised he didn't get your dad one, too."

"Are you kidding? I remember when I was little, begging for a puppy. Even looked up breeds that don't shed. My mother said something like, 'Over my dead body.' Although, from what I've heard, Angel wasn't an angel when she was young."

"Well, she's grown into the sweetest dog ever," I say as the dog kisses my hand. "So, how was school today?"

"Interesting. The entire varsity cheer team got called into the coach's office. And then we were interviewed one-on-one, which was a little nerve-racking, but I did exactly what you said to do. I told Coach that it wasn't the captain's fault, who really invited the guys, that the guys were already drunk when they got there, that they brought all the alcohol, how she tried to get them to leave, and how it got out of control."

"You told the truth," I state.

"Yep. And it felt good. She shouldn't have to get in trouble because of the other girls. Plus, the coach must have told her because, after school, she gave me a hug."

"And what about Dalton?"

"His hand is in a cast. You know what that means, right?"

"That he can't play?" I offer.

"That Chase, who's not even in high school yet, is now the second-string quarterback for the high school team. A guy in my class told me that the coach wants to make Chase practice with them. Although, I don't think he or my brother will like that."

"Damon was trying to talk the high school coach into letting him on the team, too."

"That sounds like him," she says with a laugh.

"You didn't tell me how your night was on Saturday. Did you and Chase have fun?"

She lets out a content little sigh and clasps her hands together. "Did you see how he decorated everything? It was beautiful. And our dinner—did you know about it? I can't believe I've known him my whole life, and I never knew about their family tradition. Now, I want a bucket of chicken and champagne every time we celebrate."

"Did you dance?"

"Yeah. Mostly, we talked. We talk about everything."

"That's sweet."

"It is. He's my best friend, but the guys at school are …"

"Older?" I reply.

"And they drive."

"How does Chase feel about you dating someone else?"

She sighs. "He says any guy I date had better treat me right. He thinks he has a say in that, but he doesn't. I can date anyone I want."

"I hope you'd only want to date guys who treat you right."

"That's the goal," she says. "And there's this guy I kinda have a crush on. He's older, he drives a motorcycle, and he's so sexy. His name is Matt. He asked for my number today at lunch and has been texting me all day."

"Isn't that the guy who was all over you at the eighth grade football game?"

"Yeah." She beams. "I guess he likes me."

"But Jadyn said he's not a good guy."

"Auntie Jay doesn't know him like I do," she replies as Chase and Damon barrel through the front door, followed by Haley. "And you'd better not tell anyone. Besides, it's not like I can do anything. I'm grounded for life. I don't even get to go to Dad's game tonight."

"You're still here," Chase says to me in greeting.

"Yeah, I decided it might be fun to go to the game tonight. Danny left me a ticket."

"Sweet." He glances at my clothes and sees that I'm still in my running gear. "Um, you might want to change. If you need a team shirt to wear, I can get you one of my mom's. She's going to be home at five thirty, and we're supposed to be ready to leave as soon as she gets here. We'll eat dinner at the stadium."

Angel ditches me for Chase, and the kids all declare that they have to get downstairs and get their homework done.

I FIGURE I'D better do as Chase said and get ready. I run up to my room, stopping briefly to smell the gorgeous roses before I hop in the shower.

Soon, I'm standing in front of the closet, trying to decide on what to wear. I think back to what I wore to the Nebraska game years ago and compare that to what Danny's wife was wearing to a middle school football game—which crosses such a wide spectrum, it's no help. So, I do what any normal person would do. I ask Google what pro football players' wives wear to games. I find a photo of a famous model who is married to a quarterback and peruse some of her photos, and I decide that Lori was a tad overdressed. I look in the closet again, grabbing a pair of black jeans, tall black boots, and a red plaid shirt, and I throw them on.

When I look in the mirror, I feel a little like a lumberjack.

I'm considering changing when my phone rings. I cringe when I see Jason's name.

"Hey," I say.

"Look, Jennifer," he says, "I'm just going to lay it on the line. I don't know where you are hiding out, but I need you to come back. You've got to help me talk Troy into going to rehab."

"He hasn't gone yet?"

"No. He says, without you in his life, why bother? That his life is shit. I got a call from the hotel bar the two of you used to frequent."

"Why did they call you?"

"Because he was wrecked, and they wanted someone to come get him."

"Celebrities get drunk there all the time."

"Yeah, not like this. He was drunk. High. Saying he wanted his life to end. They probably didn't want to risk a lawsuit. I've canceled his next few gigs, but we're getting into the busy season here. He's got a huge New Year's Eve party in Vegas. It's been sold out for months. I need him dried out—at least for that. If you can get him to commit to sixty days in rehab, then I can pull him out and take him to Vegas myself."

"Jason, you just need to tell him all that. I can't do it. Not again."

"I can make excuses to get him out of his other contracts, but if I cancel on Vegas for New Year's Eve, he won't work there again. They were getting ready to offer him residency at one of the big clubs. He'd do two weekends there a month. It's what you've been wanting—for him not to travel so much. It means, you could finally settle down. Have some kids."

"Maybe you didn't understand when I told you before, but I'll say it again. I'm done, Jason. I'm absolutely not getting back together with him. I can't. And if you think I'm going to have kids with him, you're as crazy as he is."

"Fine. You live your life however you want. But please, lie to him. Tell him whatever you have to. Just get him to rehab. You were together for years and supposedly loved him. Don't you owe him this?"

"All you saw were the two big crashes that made the tabloids and forced him to go to rehab. But don't think that was the extent of it. It was a constant battle just to keep him relatively sober. A battle that I didn't often win. I wouldn't have put up with it if I hadn't loved him."

"Prove it," he challenges.

I don't reply because I can't. I know, if I open my mouth, I'll agree. Not out of love for Troy, but guilt.

"Where are you anyway?" he asks.

"I'm not telling you that. But I'll think about it."

"Don't think about it too long, or he might end up dead. Yes, I'm worried about the contracts, but mostly, I'm worried about him. This is bad. Really, really bad. And I've known him for longer than you have."

"Bye, Jason."

I hang up the phone and find it hard to breathe, feeling like I just got the wind knocked out of me.

I once thought I was having a heart attack. I had just come home after hours of being with Troy at the hospital. Of taking care of him and telling him it would all be okay. That'd we'd get through it. But as soon as I got home, I felt like I was going to die.

My friend called a doctor, who came to have a look at me, checked my heart, and told me it was stress. My friend told me that it was my body's way of telling me that I was making the wrong decision regarding Troy. That I knew deep down I should leave him. That our relationship wasn't a good one. She even told me, if I chose him again, we wouldn't be friends anymore. That she couldn't deal with the drama I was bringing on myself.

I feel like it's happening again. That I can't breathe.

I take deep breaths, trying to calm myself. Tell myself it will be okay.

My phone buzzes with a text.

Jason: *Please just think about it.*

I grab my handbag and run downstairs, putting the text and Troy out of my mind as I decide to take Chase up on the offer to borrow something of his mom's.

When I get to the laundry room and am about ready to enter the kitchen, I find Jadyn and Phillip standing at the island, having what appears to be an intense discussion.

"Don't take no for an answer," Jadyn says to him.

"You don't think I'm being unreasonable?" Phillip asks, looking stressed.

Jadyn reaches out and touches his face. "It's your company, Phillip. That's why you didn't take any of the other jobs you have been offered over the years. You want to be your own boss."

"Yeah, you're right. I guess tonight will be interesting."

"Our life always is," she says, kissing him.

Their kiss is interrupted by a ringing phone that Phillip answers, so I come out of the laundry room.

"I heard you were still here," Jadyn says very matter-of-factly. She doesn't seem mad, but she also doesn't seem happy.

"Yeah, I'm sorry I didn't address that with you before. Danny and I had an argument the other night, and I said it out of anger. If I'm being honest, I wanted him to think that because I was hoping it would sort of spur things along. But it was dumb of me. I swear, I never would have left without thanking you for your incredible hospitality. I don't have a lot of friends, so I really"—my voice cracks as I try to hold my emotions in check—"appreciate it. And I'm sorry if I haven't told you."

She nods and then gives me a hug. "That's good to hear."

"There was a ticket left at my door from Danny. I don't know how it got there, since I thought he was at a hotel with the team."

"He came back home this morning to see the kids off to school before heading to the stadium."

"Were his kids home alone last night?"

"Although they are probably old enough, especially with us being next door, they either stay with us, his mom, or their part-time nanny comes over."

"That's good. So, I wasn't sure of what to wear. Do I look like a lumberjack?"

Jadyn laughs. "You look cute, but if you'd feel more comfortable switching to a team jersey, you can borrow one."

"Are you wearing what you have on?" I ask her, taking in her red tailored dress with matching blazer and black heels.

"I'm going to change into something a little more comfortable, but the box is often used for business. Phillip has clients coming tonight, but it's also the boys' first Monday night game."

"Does Dani get to go?"

"Danny said no since she's grounded."

I think about the boy who has been texting her and offer, "Wouldn't it be better to have her at the game than home alone?"

"That's exactly what I said. Why don't you text Danny and tell him you're coming to the game? As of a few minutes ago, he didn't know if you were."

I instantly feel bad. I should have told him I would be there. With freaking bells on. "I guess I had visions of surprising him, showing up on the sideline." I hold up the pass.

"Okay," she says, glancing at the clock. "You call Dani, tell her to get over here. I'll let Danny know I'm bringing her."

"Thanks," I say.

TEN MINUTES LATER, Jadyn is back in the kitchen, looking completely pulled together in a black silk blouse, dark skinny jeans, red wedges, a Burberry plaid scarf, and the red blazer.

I'm reconsidering my lumberjack look when she pulls a glittering red jersey from behind her back. "This might look cute under the shirt," she offers.

I slip into the bathroom, quickly changing, and discover she's right. The rhinestones that make up the team logo coordinate perfectly with the plaid and make me feel adorable—or it might be that the name *Diamond* is blazed across my back.

When I make my way into the kitchen, the babysitter has arrived, and the older kids, including Dani, are getting loaded in the car.

"Let's go!" Phillip says.

I'VE ALWAYS LOVED football, but I haven't been to many games. When we went to the Super Bowl that year, it was all about being seen for most people, not really as much about the game. Corporations seemed to have most of the skyboxes, and Troy and I were invited to one by a company that handled distribution for his production company. I never really stopped to think about what going to a game week after week would be like. *Do the families sit in the stands? Do they go to all the games? What's it like to know and love someone playing on the field week after week?*

Know and love.

Do I love Danny? Have I always loved him?

The traffic getting to the stadium isn't that bad for us. The parking lots are already packed full of tailgaters even though a cold front blew in this afternoon, bringing the temperature down to a cold-to-me forty degrees. Team flags are flying. Fans are decked out in team colors. Grills are smoking with barbecued food, causing my mouth to water the second we get out of the car.

We enter the stadium through doors indicating something called a Signature suite, and soon, we are in a box with an amazing view of the still mostly-empty stadium.

I find myself passing by the private restroom, fully stocked bar, and delectable-smelling buffet before standing in front of the glass.

The calm before the storm, I think.

"It's really beautiful, isn't it?" Dani says, coming to stand next to me. "My dad isn't sure about my love for football sometimes, but he has no idea what it's like to watch him take a hit. Even so, this stadium has always been an almost magical place for me. My mom didn't let me come to games much when I was a kid. Said it wasn't a place for children. Of course, Phillip and Jadyn didn't have a box back then. When I did get to come, I was always a really good girl because I wanted to come back."

"Is it hard, being his daughter?" I ask her.

She nods. "Sometimes. Like, if he has a bad game, which thankfully isn't that often, the kids at school complain about him. It's not always directed to me, but I still hear it. Sometimes, it feels like a lot to live up to. Like, I have no idea what I want to do with my life."

"You're only fourteen. You don't have to know that yet."

"Chase and my brother know what they want to do," she says with a sigh. "They know where they want to go to college. What they want to major in. Well, Damon says he wants to major in the female anatomy."

"And what about Chase?"

"He wants a business degree. Of course, they both hope to play in the professional league someday, but Damon isn't as concerned about having something to fall back on as Chase is."

"He sounds very mature for his age."

"He is in some ways. Like, he's not afraid of anything. I still can't believe he walked into a high school party like he did. But then, with other things, he's kind of naive."

"Like what?"

"The way the world works. The way high school works. He thinks he can just show up and study, and it will all fall into place. He says I shouldn't be concerned about what people think of me. And maybe I'm shallow, but I do care. I want people to like me."

"I always wanted people to like me, too. I think that's part of why I wanted to be an actress. I like to entertain. Because my father was an alcoholic, I often had to pretend like I was okay when I wasn't. I acted most my life without even realizing it. It became second nature to me."

"Kind of like football is with my dad. He was good at it when he was young, and he loved the game. There was really no conscious choice on his part. He says it was just always his goal to be the best that he could be, regardless of the level he was playing at. I'm friends with a girl whose dad played. He hurt his knee one too many times, had to retire, and became depressed. I was worried about that when my dad hurt his shoulder, but he took it as a challenge."

"Sounds like you respect your father," I state.

"I do. I still don't understand what happened with him and Mom. How Mom could just leave him for Richard. Now, *that* he took really hard. He tried to put up a front for us kids, but I think he was more worried about us than himself. I'm glad he's redoing the house. It feels better now. More like the kind of home you want to run to rather than run away from."

"Do you not get along with your mom?"

"She's very demanding," she says, looking up at the sky, searching for the right words. "She likes things to be perfect. The problem is that I'm not perfect, no matter how hard I try. My back handsprings are never straight enough. My grades are never up to par with what she got when she was in school. She's going to go ballistic if she hears about this weekend. And I'm sure she will. Being a cheer mom is one thing she's really good at. It's like she's living her life again through me. Only this time, it's going to be perfection."

"Why do you say that?"

"I know she got good grades in school, but she wasn't a cheerleader. She didn't hang out with the popular crowd."

"So, she pushes you to do that?"

"Yeah. She told me I should stop hanging around with my brother and Chase all the time. And it's not like I didn't have friends. It's just that they were all cheer-team friends. When I made varsity, they decided I was too good for them. I don't feel that way at all."

"Have you told them that?"

"Yeah, but it doesn't matter. Today, at school, they were talking behind my back, totally knowing I could hear them, about how my eighth grade boyfriend dragged me out of the party."

"They didn't think that was cool?"

"Are you kidding? He took me away from the guy they all crush on. The guy I crushed on, too." She shakes her head. "Whatever. I keep reminding myself, it's just high school. But I've also been looking into self-paced study programs and private schools. I'm not sure I'm cut out for all this drama."

"There's drama in life everywhere," I tell her. "You just have to remember what's important to you."

A big voice booms from behind us.

"That would be Tripp," Dani says with a laugh. "I should be polite and go say hello to him. He's been around a lot since he's been working with Auntie Jay. Plus, I'm starved."

I stay in my spot, watching the seats fill up and the inside of the stadium become abuzz with energy.

Jadyn comes up next to me and says, "I'm not mad at you."

"What?" I say, not sure how long I've been standing here. "I was just watching everything."

She wraps her arm around my shoulders and stares out with me. "It is pretty cool to watch. I miss being down in the stands, all bundled up against the cold. The team should be coming out onto the field shortly. Would you like me to take you down there, or are you okay with going with the kids? They know the way."

"With the kids. I didn't know Tripp would be here."

"I called him about the hotel. He said we needed to talk about it—tonight. Great guy, but he can be a little demanding. I told him I was busy. He invited himself. Not that he doesn't have his own box, but whatever. I can watch the game and chirp in his ear about what I want to do." She looks in his direction and laughs. "Maybe ply him with a few drinks and get him to sign on the dotted line."

I MEET UP with the kids and follow them down to the field. They walk the sideline, stopping along the way to give a high five or get a pat on the back from different players and staff members. None of them stop long enough to be introduced or chat. I recognize the players' looks; it's what I call *being in the zone*. When I'm shooting a movie and really into the character, it's hard for me to stop and talk to people as myself. Even though the director yells cut, I'm thinking about the next emotion, the next scene, the next line. I assume they are doing the same.

Now, I sort of wish I weren't down here. I should have told Danny I was coming. Not surprise him right before the game.

But then I spot him. He throws a warm-up pass and then turns in my direction. I should say *our* direction, but when I saw him out there, throwing the ball, I stopped in my tracks to watch. I think the kids kept going.

Our eyes meet, and it feels like time stops, the noise of one of the loudest stadiums in the country fading away. I'm rooted in my spot as I watch him stride toward me. He's dressed in his uniform from the waist down, those tight-fitting pants filling my mind with dirty thoughts. Covering his broad chest is a compression shirt that shows off all his muscles.

"Hey," he says as he comes to stand in front of me.

"Hey is for horses," I blurt out, causing him to laugh.

He stops laughing and then takes my hand like he's shaking it, meeting me for the first time. "There are a lot of cameras around," he stresses. "But I'm really glad you decided to stay."

"I'm sorry for what I said the other night. It was just me being silly, remembering what I said that night we met. I don't want you for just one night, Danny. I want so much more than that. And I'm sorry I threatened to go back to LA. I was hurt and sort of lashing out."

"I didn't mean to hurt you. Can we talk about it tomorrow when I can focus?"

"Depends," I say with a grin.

"On what?" he says, letting go of my hand.

"On if I get to see you tonight after the game."

"It's a date," he says as the kids join us.

He gives them high fives while they offer words of advice.

When they take off, I lean in and whisper, "And be sure to watch your backside. I know I will be."

THE GAME IS exciting, exhilarating, and slightly terrifying.

Danny was bragging about his offensive line when we watched the film, but the defender he was worried about the most has broken through the line for two sacks already.

After a vicious third sack, Danny lies on the ground for a few seconds, not moving.

"Is he okay?" I ask Phillip, grabbing on to his shirtsleeve in a panic.

He watches the replay. "Yeah, looks like he got caught in the ribs with the helmet. Probably knocked the wind out of him."

"Will he be able to keep playing?"

"Danny? Uh, yeah. If you're around tomorrow and, you know, not going back to LA, maybe he'll show you all of his bruises."

"I'm not going back," I say. "Will he be sore?"

"Oh, yeah. It will be hard for him to get out of bed. He'll probably spend the morning at the stadium, being treated."

"But I thought Tuesdays were his days off."

"They usually are, but since they are playing tonight and then again on Thursday, it's a short week. Hopefully, they figure out a way to stop that guy."

"Yeah," I say as Danny finally pops up off the ground in what was probably the longest ten seconds of my life.

AT HALFTIME, I decide to eat from the buffet that's set up. And the food is delicious. I really should have eaten earlier, but I was nervous. I'm shoving food in my mouth when Tripp sits down next to me.

"I hear you don't think I should tear down the hotel. Do you really think that Jadyn can make it a place that will attract you? Make celebrities like you want to stay there?"

"Have you ever been to her house? Have you seen what she's done to Danny's house?"

"No, I haven't."

"Not even her office over the garage?"

"No. But I have seen a lot of her commercial work."

"If I had your money, Tripp, I would tell Jadyn to make the hotel feel like her home. Let her make it personal. Warm, inviting, and luxurious. The kind of place where you can curl your feet up on a chair, look out the window to enjoy a few moments of peace from your chaotic life, and sleep like a baby in the most comfortable bed you've ever felt. Tell her to throw in the delectable and healthy warm cookies she gives her kids before bedtime, and everyone in the world is going to want to stay there."

"I asked her to fly to LA with me tomorrow to present her new ideas to my board. She refused. Apparently, tomorrow is Halloween. Trick-or-treating and all that."

"That's a big holiday for kids. Didn't you go get candy when you were young?"

"Yeah, we'd run around the neighborhood with pillowcases until they were full and then go home and eat candy until we were sick. She's coming on Wednesday instead. I have a favor. Would you consider joining us? Talking to the board about what celebrities are looking for. Really, if you would repeat what you just said to me, I think we could convince them."

"Does that mean you are considering a renovation?"

"I can't believe that I am, but yes." He glances back at Jadyn. "She's hard to say no to. It'd be tough to be her husband."

"Phillip seems pretty happy," I counter.

"Yes, he does. It makes me hate him a little. I'm trying to buy his company."

"Because you hate him?"

"No, because he understands how to run a good business, values his employees, maintains a healthy bottom line, and has only fulfilled a portion of its potential. That's what I do. I take good companies, infuse them with cash, make them great, and then reap the profits."

"Sometimes, it's not about reaping the profits," I mutter as Danny throws a beautiful pass straight into the arms of a receiver for a touchdown. "Sometimes, it's about the beauty of the game."

Tripp slides his hand on top of mine. "I understand you're newly single. Would you have dinner with me sometime?"

"Like a date?"

"Yes, like a date. My favorite restaurant in the world is in Paris. I'd love to take you."

"Um, I, uh," I stutter.

I haven't been asked on a date in a long time. With Danny, it's different. I can't tell him I'm seeing Danny. I mean, I want to be seeing Danny, but I have no idea what we are doing. I guess we had a date last night.

"Jennifer," Jadyn yells out, motioning for me to join her.

I excuse myself from my seat without giving Tripp an answer and take the stairs up to the lounge area of the suite.

"Was Tripp hitting on you?"

"He wants to take me to Paris for dinner. He also wants me to go to LA with you and talk to his board from a celebrity's perspective."

"I told him you were going through something personal and that I wasn't going to ask you to do that."

"It's the least I can do," I say, the guilt washing over me. "I should probably go back and deal with life there, too."

Danny

AFTER THE GAME is over, I consider texting Jennifer from the locker room and asking if she'd like to come down. I know the guys would love to meet her. I imagine wrapping my arm around her and proudly introducing her to everyone. But, as usual, there are reporters in here as well. And none of them know that I'm about to announce my divorce. In less than forty-eight hours, I will be able to take Jennifer out in public. I can shower her with attention anywhere and everywhere.

If she wants it.

Most of the time, it seems like she does.

And I was shocked at how devastated I felt when she said she was leaving. That girl has no idea how hard it is for me to keep her at arm's length. I thought having her here, hanging out with her, and getting to know her would maybe make me like her less. That, over the years, I put her so far up on a pedestal in my mind that she could never live up to it.

But she's added scaffolding and built that pedestal even higher than I could have imagined. She's my dream and so much more. Not only is she very real, she's funny and freaking adorable.

I go through the motions of my postgame routine. Speak to reporters, sign autographs, do the press conference, congratulate the team. I know that Jadyn and Phillip have already gone home in order to try to get the kids to bed since it's a school night. It was a big deal that Chase and Damon were allowed to come.

I walk out to my car to find the girl who's been on my mind all day leaning against my old truck.

"I was looking for your Ferrari. I thought all top athletes drove their hottest cars on game day."

"Not me," I say. "I've never driven it to the stadium. I drive this instead."

"And why's that?" she asks.

"Tradition, maybe."

"Oh, boy. Are you one of those guys who won't change his socks all season?"

"Sometimes." I laugh. "But this isn't like that. I drove this Tahoe in college. Drove it to the stadium the first time I visited after I signed. I've driven it to every game since. It's not a superstition though. It's more about remembering how far I've come. The guy who took off for college in this truck had big dreams. The guy who got drafted to a professional team had even bigger ones."

"And the guy who drives it now still has an empty wall to fill," she says, completely understanding me.

I take a step closer to her, feeling awestruck. My wife chastised me for keeping my old truck. She bitched when I put a new motor in it to keep it running. She didn't get why it was important. Jennifer understood after only a few sentences.

In that moment, I don't give a shit who might see. I lower my lips to hers.

"This kiss," she murmurs, "it reminds me of that night. It wasn't deep, yet it wasn't chaste. It wasn't long, yet it felt like it lasted forever. It's exactly the same as it was on the beach—profoundly fierce yet achingly, heartbreakingly soft."

"That's how I felt. Like my heart was literally breaking, knowing I couldn't do what felt so right. What still feels so right." I lead her around to the passenger side and open the door for her.

When we get home, I walk her up the stairs and to her door.

"Want to come in for a nightcap?" she asks.

I know the last thing either of us wants is a drink. I also know, based on the ugly bruises forming on my ribs and shoulder from the sacks I took, I'm going to be sore as heck tomorrow.

I pick her up, carry her over the threshold, through Jadyn's office, and straight to her bedroom. She's got her arms around my neck, holding me tight, and our lips move in a fervent kiss as I lie on top of her on the bed.

She pulls off my suit jacket as I'm tugging off her shirt and undoing her bra, knowing nothing is going to stop us. Our naked chests touch, igniting a passion in me I thought I'd grown out of. An uncontrollable lust-filled need. I'm devouring her lush lips, roughly running my hands across her beautiful breasts, slipping my hand down her pants—

Ring, ring.

I barely register the noise. The feel of her trembling under my touch has set my body aflame. I can see the goal line. The finish. The big score.

Ring, ring.

"Danny," she says, pulling her lips away from mine, "don't you think you should answer it? It might be the kids."

I kiss her again, trying to wish away the noise.

Ring, ring.

I sigh loudly and get off the bed, my body aching the second our skin stops touching. I pick my jacket off the floor and pat it down, looking for my phone, as it rings again.

"Dad!" Devaney says when I answer, sounding like she's crying. "I was worried sick about you! Why didn't you answer?"

"I, uh—" I say, my mind coming up blank, mostly because my eyes are focused on Jennifer, topless, lying across the bed.

"Whatever. You should be home by now."

"Are you crying?" I ask, trying to assess the seriousness of her situation versus the seriousness of mine.

"Yes, I am. Because Mom just called from Bermuda and lost it. She found out about the party from one of the cheer moms. I don't think she knows everything, but she's very angry."

"Well, Dani, what you did—"

"Yeah, no. She's not just mad at me. She said some really

hateful things about you. That's why I'm crying. How come you aren't home yet? I *need* you to be home."

"I'll be right there," I tell her, ending the call.

I close my eyes and let out a sigh.

Topless Jennifer sits up, quickly pulling on her shirt. "Is she okay?"

"She's upset. Lori found out about the party." I glance at my phone and see the other two calls were from her. "Yelled at her. Apparently said some hateful things about me. I need to go calm her down."

"Do you want me to come with you?"

"We'd probably better call it a night. I'm sorry."

"It's okay, Danny. For whatever it's worth, I had fun tonight. Thank you for inviting me to the game."

"Thank you for not leaving," I tell her.

"Are we still hanging out tomorrow?" she asks as she walks me out. "Phillip said you'd probably have to get therapy or something."

"I will in the morning, but I'll pick you up around eleven. We'll have lunch and then shop."

"Sounds like a plan," she says, pulling me to her lips for a really wonderful good-night kiss.

OCTOBER 31ST

Jennifer

I WAKE UP to more texts from Troy. I know I should block his number and forget about him, but I can't pretend like he doesn't exist.

> **Troy:** *If you come home, I'll go to rehab.*
>
> **Me:** *You need to go, no matter what I do. Rehab is for you.*
>
> **Troy:** *No, I'd be doing it for you. You're my light, remember?*
>
> **Me:** *Have you seen the video footage of yourself at the brothel?*
>
> **Troy:** *No.*
>
> **Me:** *You should watch it. Then maybe you would understand why I don't want to come home. And pay close attention to what you said when one of the girls asked you about your Eddy tattoo.*

I get up and get myself ready. I want to look amazing for my day with Danny but still casual. I end up with a cute graphic tee, skinny jeans tucked into boots, and a blazer.

> **Troy:** *I watched it. I get that you're mad. I would be, too. But it was a mistake. It didn't mean anything.*

Me: *That's where you are wrong. If you can't understand that, then I didn't mean anything to you either.*

I set my phone to vibrate and then go downstairs to wait for Danny.

"Hey, Angel," I say as she kisses my hand in greeting and wags her tail. "How's my new best friend today? Let's go sit in our spot, shall we?"

I grab a cup of coffee, see a note from Jadyn that she'll be at school parties most of the day, and head to the study. Angel follows me, choosing to lie in front of the windows in the sunshine.

I close my eyes and try to decide what to do. I'm going back to LA tomorrow. I probably need to find myself somewhere to live. The question is, do I see Troy or not? Should I help him get to rehab? Make promises I have no intention of keeping for his own good? Or would that just be setting him up for failure?

Jason: *You told him to watch the video?!*

Me: *Yeah, maybe if he sees what rock bottom looks like to the rest of us, he'll want to go to rehab. That's what you want, right?*

Jason: *He's sobbing. On the floor, sobbing. I don't know what to do with him.*

Me: *Neither do I. Maybe it's time we stop being his crutch. Maybe he still hasn't hit bottom yet. It's his life. At some point, he's going to have to decide what he wants to do with it.*

Jason: *I ordered a new car with my cut of Vegas.*

Me: *So, you don't really care about him ... or me. Don't message me again, Jason.*

I close my eyes, trying to shut out the world.

A short time later, the front door opens, and Danny hobbles in.

"Are you okay?" I ask.

"Yeah, this is what the day after a game looks like." He pulls his shirt up and shows me a massive bruise over his ribs.

"Danny! That looks horrible." I leap out of my chair and kneel in front of him, gently touching the contusion. "Are your ribs broken?"

"No, just bruised. Hurts like a bitch, but it will be fine in time for the next game."

He stares down at me. I look up and realize, well, that I'm kneeling in front of him. In perfect position to unzip his jeans and give him a big sideline blow—or whatever that term was that made me laugh. I start to rise, but then a tattoo catches my eye. As I stand, I pull his shirt up a little further. Down his side are letters spelling out his last name, the font including a diamond shape. I allow my finger to trace over each and every letter.

"What else do you have?" I purr.

He starts to take off his shirt but then groans. "You're going to have to help me. I should have worn a button-up today. Easier to get in and out of."

I raise my hand. "If you need a volunteer, I'm happy to help you get undressed. You know, since you are injured and all."

He laughs as I gently tug his shirt up over his head. I don't see any on his front, so I shuffle behind him, trailing my finger across the top of his jeans along the way. On his shoulder is a bold red *N*.

I read the words inside it.

"That's the end of the prayer the Nebraska players say before each game." He recites the entire poem in his normal voice, but when he gets to the part that is tattooed, he starts speaking louder, chanting it out, "Can't be beat! Won't be beat!"

"I like it," I say, taking the time to admire his back in all its chiseled glory. "Any more?"

He holds out his left arm, so I continue to circle him, thinking of a show I used to watch where witches would circle a man in order to cast an effective spell on him, usually one that involved his love and passionate desires. I sigh, wishing I had such talents.

His left bicep is tattooed with the word *Champs* in script as well as the Roman numerals of the year of his first win and the Lombardi Trophy encased in swirls. Toward the bottom is another banner indicating his second win.

"Do you have plans for more?"

He flips his wrist, showing me that my marker-written name is nearly gone. "Maybe I should make it permanent."

My heart flutters at the thought of seeing my name tattooed on him. I go into the kitchen, grab a permanent marker from a drawer, and proceed to re-sign his arm.

"I love it," he says, although the way he says it makes me feel like he just told me he was in love with me. "I suppose we'd better get going if we want to have lunch before our appointment."

HE TAKES ME to a busy restaurant outside of an upscale mall. We sit at the bar, order a drink and some food, and chat.

"I come here a lot," he says. "They have the best crab cakes. When I sit at the bar, with my back toward the restaurant, usually, no one really notices me."

"What happened last night? Did you call your wife?"

"No way. I got Dani calmed down and collapsed in bed. It was late; I wasn't going to deal with Lori. She can tell me whatever was so important tomorrow when we sign the papers. Besides, I'm pretty sure she texted me everything she wanted to say."

"Was she mad?"

"Of course, and the party was clearly all my fault," he says with a laugh.

When our drinks are served, he toasts to orange roses, Halloween, and me.

I really don't remember much of the rest of lunch other than the intensity in which he looked at me. The rest didn't really matter.

After lunch, we drive a short distance to a kitchen design center.

While we're waiting for our salesperson, I say, "Do you have to change your backsplash?"

"I guess not. Why?"

"I don't know. It reminds me of the ocean, and I think it's pretty."

"Do you think I should leave the kitchen as is?" he asks.

"Well, I'd definitely get rid of the electric-blue color and all the peacock-ness."

"Jadyn told me to look around and see if I fall in love with anything." He stops in his tracks and gazes into my eyes. "I think I just found it," he says, the corners of his mouth pulling into a little smirk. "Can I install you in my kitchen?"

"That sounds so old-fashioned," I tease. "You want me barefoot and pregnant, too?"

The smirk turns to a full-on grin. "Not a bad idea." He stops again and shakes his head. "This is all so backward."

"What is?" I ask.

"Us," he says.

The designer's eyes get big when she sees me. "Um, Jennifer Edwards," she says with a stutter, "I wasn't expecting you."

"I'm in town, visiting Jadyn, and since she couldn't come with Danny today, Halloween parties and all, she sent me."

"Oh, I see. Um, have you seen anything that you like?"

"I saw one thing that I really liked," Danny says. The second she turns her back, he flicks my hand, indicating that he meant me. Then he smiles.

The kind of adorable smile that makes me melt. *Seriously, when did I turn all girlie?*

Most of the guys I dated, it was because we became fast friends, had fun hanging out, and hooked up. Danny is the only guy who makes me feel all the things I've acted out in so many movies. The butterflies in my stomach, the goose bumps, heart beating faster, stars in my eyes, strung out on love, and feeling like I might literally die if I can't be with him. The kind of stuff fairy tales are made of—the one true love, kiss her to wake her up, live happily ever after.

The girl leads us into a smaller room where she has a computer model of Danny's kitchen now along with three different material design boards.

"Okay," she says, her professionalism returning, "in this one, Jadyn suggested a medium-gray paint on the walls, leaving your cabinets and trim white. The wood floors would be darkened, as I think you are planning to do throughout the house." She holds up a sample tile. "The backsplash has been changed to a soft gray marble to coordinate with a new gray marble countertop. Notice that the island has been painted a deep shade of gray. Industrial barstools and simple pendant lightning complete the look. What do you think?"

"I think we should see all the options before we decide," he says.

She moves us down the table to another set of samples and switches her computer rendering. "For option two, the island is stained a shade darker than the floor, the white cabinets have been given a glaze to make them look more rustic, and reclaimed wood is added to the hood area to give it more of a Tuscan farmhouse feel."

She doesn't bother asking for his opinion this time, but right now, I'm sort of loving the farmhouse look.

"In the third option, the island has been painted what I'm told is the same blue-green as your study." She holds up a sample tile. In this version, the backsplash has been replaced with the most gorgeous tiles I think I've ever seen in my life, causing me to gasp.

"It's beautiful, isn't it?" she says. "Ribbons of mother of pearl are swirled into a pure white marble. In this mock-up, it runs all the way to the ceiling behind the hood, which has been replaced with an industrial wood and metal version."

The result is glamorous, casual, and cozy. *Is there such a thing as industrial glam?*

"Which one do you like best?" I ask Danny, trying not to influence him.

But I know this; I will be begging Jadyn to help me design wherever I end up living. My heart skips a beat at the thought of this kitchen being our kitchen, of raising a family with him, and of giving up the lifestyle I have had. Part of me worries about giving something up for a man. Regardless of if I end up with Danny, someone else, or by myself, I'm ready to slow down. I'm ready to start a family.

Danny goes back to study each mock-up. Finally, he points to the last one and says, "I like certain elements of each design, but I love this one. Love that the tile is a little flashy but is toned down by the rustic industrial elements. And that island color is my favorite." He turns to me. "What do you think?"

"Well, considering I gasped over that tile, you could probably tell which one I loved. Upon closer inspection, I also like how she used the same basic color palette for everything already redone on that floor—your study and the master suite. I feel like this will continue to tie it all together."

"I guess we'll take it," Danny says.

The designer looks from me to Danny and says, "*We'll*? Are you two, like, together?"

"What?" I scoff, recovering more quickly than Danny. "I think he's referring to him and Jadyn."

"Oh," the girl says, turning a shade of red. "Of course. I just … I'll stop talking now. We have all the measurements, so we'll get it ordered. Jadyn wanted it rushed, so I'll do that straightaway."

"Awesome. Thank you," Danny says, signing the work order that she holds out to him before she slinks away.

"Let's go," I tell him, leading him out the door.

"Is it bad that I did mean we, as in you and me?" he says once we're in his car.

I melt. "Not at all."

"It just seems so strange. You've been here for less than a week, and I'm picturing you in my life, living in my house. I feel like that's how my life should have been. But it's not," he says.

He looks sad, so I decide to change the subject.

"So, it's Halloween. I know the kids have parties at school today, but what will go on tonight?"

Danny starts the car and turns to me with a sparkle in his eyes.

"Remember I told you, Halloween was always my favorite holiday as a kid? Dressing up wasn't the only reason." He's got a naughty grin on his face.

"Sounds like trouble," I say with a laugh. "Did you smash pumpkins and stuff?"

"Oh no, that would be disrespectful. But we might have TPed a few homes. Possibly forked their yards and might have Fruity Pebbled a few sidewalks."

"TPed? You mean, like toilet-papered houses? I've never done that before."

"Never?" he asks, shocked.

"Nope."

"Oh, boy. You're going to have fun tonight." He glances at the clock. "Hmm. It's getting late. I was thinking it would be fun to make homemade pizzas with the kids before they go trick-or-treating. When I was young, we used to make them in pumpkin shapes and decorate them to look like jack-o'-lanterns. But I need to go to the store to get supplies for tonight."

"Why don't I start the pizzas with the kids, and you go to the store? By the time you get back, we can eat."

He reaches over, takes my hand in his, and gives it a little squeeze. "That sounds like an awesome idea."

WE GET BACK to Danny's house as the kids are getting home from school.

"How was school?" Danny asks them as we all meet up in the kitchen.

"A couple of my teachers brought treats in for Halloween, but it sucks, not having parties like we did in grade school." Damon pouts.

"I'm over all that," Dani says with a roll of her eyes.

"Well, how would you feel about us making homemade pizzas tonight?" I ask them.

"I'm all for pizza, all the time," Damon says, his pout quickly replaced with a grin much like his father's.

Danny pulls his phone out and shows us all a photo. "I had your grandma send me this today," he says. "When I was a kid, we used to make pizzas for Halloween and decorate them like jack-o'-lanterns."

"That's kinda lame," Dani says, but she's smiling, too.

"But tasty," Danny counters. "Jennifer is going to help you make the dough. I have to run an errand but will be back shortly. I say we have a contest for the best-looking pizza."

"And who's going to judge that?" Damon asks.

"Grandma," Devaney answers. "She loves me."

"I will agree to sending Grandma pictures and letting her judge, but we are not allowed to tell her whose is whose. Deal?"

"What do we win?" Damon wonders.

"If I win, I'm not grounded, and I get to go trick-or-treating with Chase. He's taking Madden and Ryder."

"Devaney, you can go with Chase to do that regardless of if

you win," Danny says sweetly. "Wanting to help the little kids is nice of you."

"Does that mean, after we've worn them out, I can go over to—"

"Don't push it," Danny says firmly.

She rolls her eyes again but doesn't argue further.

I shoo Danny out of the kitchen. Once he leaves for the store, the kids and I mix up the dough. While it's rising in the warming drawer, I chop up veggies and show Devaney how to sauté them. Damon is in charge of cooking the ground sausage.

"We need some music," Devaney says. She eyes me seriously. "Do you listen to Dad's kind of music?"

"What does your dad listen to?" I ask, realizing I don't know.

"Rock mostly," she says.

"Do you not like that kind of music?" I ask.

"Well, I might if the music he listened to in college wasn't, like, a million years ago."

"I like a lot of music," I tell her as I sprinkle flour all over one side of the island and set up all the toppings on the other side. "Pick whatever you like." What she likes is dance music, which is awesome because it's my favorite, too.

I get the dough out of the warming drawer, roll it into individual balls, and set them in the flour. The kids are rolling it out when the front door bursts open.

I look up, expecting Danny, but see his wife instead. She doesn't appear to notice us, just marches up the stairs, seemingly on a mission.

The kids' eyes are as big as saucers, but neither one of them seems surprised when a loud scream breaks the silence that fell over the kitchen when she walked in.

"Oh, boy," Devaney says. "Mom doesn't sound happy."

And she's right.

Lori flies down the stairs and finally notices the three of us in the kitchen. Her face is red when she marches to the island and glares at me. "What are you doing here? Where is my husband?" she demands.

"He is running a quick errand—"

"Well, aren't you all cozy? Here in my house, with my children. Making a mess of *my* kitchen."

"Um, we're just making pizzas. Would you like to join us?"

She gets an amused look on her face. "Join you? In *my* house? Yes, I think I would. This is actually a little surreal, I will admit. Another woman cooking in my kitchen."

"Did you cook a lot?" I ask, knowing full well that she didn't, based on the stove.

"What? No. A chef prepared our meals for us. It's all too messy."

I purposely splash a little sauce on the counter. "Yeah, it is. Kinda like life."

"Mom," Damon says, "we're having a contest to make the best jack-o'-lantern pizza. Grandma Diamond is going to judge which one wins. Daddy used to do it when he and Uncle Phillip and Auntie Jay were young. How come we never did this before?"

Lori does a long blink, seemingly trying to keep her anger in check. "I don't know, honey. We'll have to ask your father that." She turns to her daughter. "I'm also here to talk to your father about what went on Friday night at the party. I've heard more of the story since I arrived home from Bermuda. Why didn't you tell me what happened? That you were at a party where police were present?"

"I had already left," Devaney says.

"Oh, yes. I heard how your stupid friendship with Chase caused the quarterback on the team you are supposed to be supporting to break his hand."

"It wasn't Chase's fault," she starts to say, but her mother doesn't let her finish.

"You are not allowed to see him anymore."

"What?" Devaney says, the hurt in her eyes apparent.

"I'm thinking maybe you didn't hear the whole story," I say, standing up for Chase. "He went there—"

Lori aims her finger and venom at me. "Don't you even think about telling me anything about my daughter. As a matter of fact, why don't you get your husband-stealing whore ass out of my house?"

"Lori!" Danny says, his voice booming through the commotion.

I didn't even hear him come in.

She marches straight up to him. "Don't even start with me, Danny Diamond," she says, her voice dripping with disgust. "You left our children with a complete stranger."

"She's not a stranger."

"And what did you do to my house? I came over to pick up some clothes. Where is my stuff?"

"I moved the bedrooms around," Danny says calmly in what seems to be a well-practiced tone. "The personal items you left here were boxed up and put into a storage unit."

"You put all my clothing into a storage unit? If they get ruined, you're replacing them!"

"The storage unit is high-end and very suitable for your needs. Your items are also insured, should there be any damage." He opens a drawer in the kitchen and pulls out an envelope. "The address and key to the unit are in here."

"Why are you still here?" she asks me.

"I'm still here because Danny invited me, and I'm not leaving his house until he asks me to."

Danny

LORI TURNS TO me. "You don't think it's a coincidence that I go out of town, you bring this whore into my house, and our daughter goes to a party and is drinking? It's your fault. Were you even caring for our children while I was gone? Or were you too busy whoring around?"

What she says hits home, and I immediately feel guilty. I was making out with Jennifer and almost ignored Phillip's call.

"Are you saying that you wouldn't have let Devaney go to the cheer sleepover?" I ask Lori.

"That has nothing to do with it," she says.

"Yeah, it does. Maybe you didn't get the whole story. Maybe, instead of listening to cheer-mom gossip from women whose girls weren't even at the party, you should have asked me or your daughter about it. It's not as simple as you make it sound."

She crosses her arms in front of her chest. "Enlighten me."

Devaney, who surprisingly hasn't left the room and is standing close to Jennifer, like she's her backup, tells her side of things. She leaves out quite a bit, but I get it.

Once she finishes, I tell Lori the rest.

"You're telling me that, rather than call her own father, she called Chase? And Phillip didn't call you to go get our daughter because he knew you were with your whore."

"I'm not a whore," Jennifer says adamantly. "Stop saying that."

"Why don't you go home, Jennifer?" I suggest, wanting to protect her from the drama with Lori.

The second I see Lori's smirk, I realize I played right into her hand.

"Yeah, why don't you leave?" Lori repeats.

Jennifer drops a towel on the counter and looks me dead in the eyes. "You know what? I'm sorry your wife barged in while you were gone, and I invited her to join us. Enjoy your pizzas."

My heart feels like it's breaking all over again when she walks out. I want to run and stop her from leaving, hold her in my arms and apologize for the things my wife said, but Lori starts in on me again.

"How could you leave our children alone with a stranger?" she asks.

"Let's go outside and talk," I suggest. "The kids don't need to hear all this."

"No! The kids are practically grown. They need to understand what's going on here."

"What's going on here is, I invited a friend to come over to my house. You aren't living here anymore. That was your decision, not mine." I take her arm and lead her to the front door. "It's time for you to leave."

Surprisingly, she complies. When I get her outside, I see why. Richard is waiting for her. I didn't even notice his car sitting in the street when I got home, my mind on all things Jennifer.

He gets out of the car and waves her over.

"I have to go now," Lori says, "but we are not through with this conversation."

"I'll see you tomorrow at the attorney's office. We can talk all you want there, but I refuse to do it in front of the children."

"Fine," she says.

The second she is gone, I rush over to Jennifer's room. When I knock on the door, she doesn't answer. I let myself into Jadyn's office and then go knock on the bedroom door. Still, no answer. I turn the knob and peek in.

She's not there, so I go downstairs through the garage and into the Mackenzies' house. I expect to find a house filled with chaos, but it's quiet. I vaguely remember Jadyn telling me earlier that they were going out for dinner tonight before trick-or-treating.

I go to the study, knowing it's Jennifer's favorite spot, and find her sitting, curled up.

"Hey," I say. "Sorry about all that."

When she turns to me, I can see that she's been crying.

"Do you think I'm a husband-stealing whore?"

I move toward her. "What do you think?"

"No. But it rattled me. And struck a chord. Do you know how badly I did want to steal you back then?"

"How badly?" I ask as I wiggle my way into the chair with her.

"With every inch of my being," she says.

"Would you come back and finish making pizzas with us?"

"Only if she's gone," she replies.

"She's history," I say, placing my lips on hers.

WE WALK HAND in hand back to my house, make pizzas with the kids, and have a great time. It doesn't hurt that my mother chooses Jennifer's pizza as the grand-prize winner. Once dinner is over, the kids are quick to head to the Mackenzies' house.

"We'd better get out there." I hand Jennifer a bowl of candy and lead her to the front porch. I tell her to take a seat and then run into the garage to get the cooler.

"What's that for?" she asks when I return with it.

"Candy for the kids. Beer for the parents." I open the cooler, grab a bottle, wrap a koozie around it, and give it to her.

We hand out candy and beers for quite a while.

"It's really amazing, all the children in your neighborhood," she says as we get a break in the action. "And that they are all with their parents."

"It's a great place for kids to grow up," I agree.

She lets out a little sigh.

"What?"

"I have been thinking about your tattoos," she says.

"Because you haven't gotten to see them all yet?"

"I thought I had seen them all," she counters.

I shake my head, pull up the hem of my jeans, and show her my ankle. "Phillip and I have this tattoo in the same spot. Jadyn has it on her hip. It's the wing design that is on her parents' gravestones."

"That must have been really hard for all of you," she says.

I lower my head. "It was, but it made us even closer."

She leans in and gives me a sweet kiss. The smile on her face as she pulls away takes me back to that night on the beach. But I need to forget about the past and live in the present. And the present includes my wife, who said something horrible about Jennifer today. Something completely uncalled for. It's not like I'm sleeping with her.

Yet.

"Is their relationship as perfect as it seems?" Jennifer asks, interrupting my dirty thoughts.

"They get in little tiffs like anyone, but even those you can see right through. For the most part, they make their marriage a priority. They're best friends and such good partners."

"True love?" she asks.

"Definitely." I want to say something about us being true love because I believe that's what she is. My true love. But it feels awkward. And part of me still can't believe she's here. "You said you were thinking about my tattoos."

"Oh, yeah. I think you should do it. Have more kids. Fill up the empty space."

And I'm thinking that would be the most wonderful thing ever—if she'd be the one to help me do so.

THE TRICK-OR-TREATERS ARE long gone, the kids are asleep, and Jennifer and I are on our fifth house of the night. I stop spraying water onto the sidewalk and sprinkle on Fruity Pebbles while I watch her. She's running back and forth across the yard, toilet paper trailing behind her as she layers it across Joey's hedges, having the time of her life.

Even though this week has been sort of a disaster with all things Jennifer, it's been the most fun I've had in a long time. Something about her makes me feel young again. Young, happy, and more like myself. I love that I get to just be me when I'm around her. That I can say silly stuff to make her giggle instead of getting chastised. I love that we can joke around. And don't even get me started on the way kissing her feels. If things weren't so complicated, I would have done way more than that by now, and I know without a doubt that we'd have equally as much fun in bed.

I'm pulled from my thoughts when a bright light comes on.

Shit, I think, getting ready to run.

But then I see a cop has Jennifer cornered by a tree on the edge of the property.

"Whoa," he says, shining his flashlight in her face. "Are you Jennifer Edwards?"

"Yep," she says.

"Is this some kind of celebrity prank?" the cop asks. "Am I on camera?"

"Nope," I say, sneaking up behind him. "Just a couple of kids having fun."

He quickly turns in my direction, the flashlight blinding me.

"And Danny Diamond? Now, I know something's up."

"What's up," I say, "is that I was telling Jennifer about all the stuff we used to do to our friends' houses on Halloween when we were kids. And she told me that she'd never TPed a house in her life. I felt that needed to be remedied."

He shines the light back in her direction. "Is that true?"

"Your light is really bright," Jennifer says, holding her hand up. "It hurts my eyes."

"Plus, we're kind of trying to be incognito here," I add.

"Oh, well, shoot, you're right," he says, quickly turning off the torch.

"It's true," Jennifer tells him.

"I can't believe you've never done that," he says. "Hell, back in my day, I mean—"

Jennifer hands him a roll of toilet paper from the sack she has tied to her belt loop. "We've done four of his friends' houses so far. Want to know my favorite part? It's when you throw the roll as high as you can and then a branch catches it and it rolls back down so fast and it's so pretty and you catch it and then you throw it up in the air again."

The cop peers around in every direction. "Do you swear, I'm not on camera?"

"We swear," I say.

He takes the toilet paper and heaves it into the air. "Gosh, that's fun. I'll be honest, I was a bit of a hellion when I was young. Those who knew me are shocked I'm a cop. I was always having run-ins with the locals in my small town."

"Things were different back then though," I say. "The cops knew everyone. They didn't have to threaten with arrest. They just told us they were calling our parents."

"I know, right?" he says with a grin as he catches the TP and throws it back in the air. "And they'd confiscate our beer. Or make us pour it out." He grins at Jennifer as I hand him a few forks to place in the yard. "You ever get caught parking by the lake?"

"Hell," Jennifer says with a laugh, "where I grew up, all we had was a pond."

"We didn't even have that," I add. "We just pulled into a cornfield."

"I can't believe I'm reminiscing about the good ole days and committing trespassing, littering, and criminal mischief with Jennifer Edwards and Danny Diamond. Best night ever."

"Well, the good news is, it's easy to clean up," Jennifer says.

"And we're doing my house," I say, "so my friends won't know who to blame."

"Now, that there is sheer brilliance," the officer says, shaking my hand before he gets back into his car and takes off.

Jennifer and I run to the corner where we parked.

"Ohmigosh, that was such a rush," she says, pushing me against the side of my truck. "I was so imagining myself in an orange jumpsuit and a mug shot in all the papers."

"Another nice thing about living in a small town," I say, holding her eyes and enjoying the feel of her body against mine.

"Kansas City isn't small," she counters as she pats down my chest and pulls the flask out of my pocket. She takes a slug and then offers it to me.

I take a shot and then say, "No, but our neighborhood feels like a small town. That's why I was originally drawn to it."

"And how did Phillip and Jadyn end up living next door to you?" she asks as she runs her hand across the nape of my neck, causing me to instantly harden.

"It's kind of crazy now that I think back. I got drafted and bought the house. Lori wasn't thrilled with it even though it was bigger than I ever imagined. It needed remodeling, which I knew was quite an undertaking. But it was the exact location I wanted, had a panoramic lake view, and the back faced west, so we could watch the sunset. You know that Phillip and Jadyn grew up door next to each other, and when I was in sixth grade, my family moved into the neighborhood. I was a cocky little shit and wanted to play catch with Phillip. Said something about girls not being able to play football. Jadyn ran into her house in tears and then came back out, demanding to play. When I balked at the idea, she slugged me."

Jennifer covers her mouth, trying to control her giggles. "Oh, that's awesome. And let me guess; you've been best friends ever since?"

"Yep. I told you about how I took the gang to Vegas for Jadyn's and Phillip's bachelorette and bachelor parties?"

"No, you didn't. You just told me that you bought the car in Vegas."

"Phillip and Jadyn have never liked to be apart. He didn't know the girls were even there the first night. We did the typical routine with the drunk limo and strip club while the girls did a spa day and drank a lot of wine. Anyway, that was the night I bought the Ferrari, and Lori was pissed I hadn't consulted her. I know we were married and all, but I used a small portion of my sign-on bonus, which I felt was mine to spend since I'd gotten it before we were married."

"How did Phillip find out Jadyn was there?"

"Oh, that's classic. The next afternoon, I hired these masked strippers to come into our penthouse suite and made Jadyn dress like them and dance on Phillip."

"Oh my gosh. She danced and stripped in front of you all?"

"She didn't really get to the stripping part. Phillip knew it was her right away because he saw her tattoo. But Jadyn didn't think he recognized her, and she was getting mad that he was being so handsy, but he played it perfectly. I was dying. Let's just say, Jadyn would starve before she ever earned money as a stripper."

"I had a stripper fail once, too! I was in Vegas with Riley Johnson and Knox Daniels. I was so drunk, and I totally fell. Made a fool of myself." She hoots.

"I saw the video. I thought you were damn sexy, and that was before we met. Even though I'm sure it was embarrassing, it looked like a fun night."

"It was," she says with a smile. "I used to have a lot of fun. And I had fun tonight. Thank you for taking me."

"I haven't had this much fun in a long time. Although watching you in the bounce house in that little skimpy costume, jumping around, is high on the list."

She smacks my arm and then leans in to kiss me.

All of a sudden, the lights come on in Joey's house.

She says, "We're busted," against my mouth as we instinctively duck.

We watch Joey move from window to window, turning on lights, until he's in the kitchen, drinking milk from the carton.

"I don't think he knows we're out here. Good thing we parked on the corner."

As soon as the lights all turn off, we hightail it back home and decorate both my house and the Mackenzies'.

Jennifer

IT'S LATE WHEN we sneak up to my room.

Danny is barely inside the door when I say, "Is it weird that I'm here?"

"A little. It's like I'm living out a fantasy, a dream."

"Have you thought about me since we stopped talking?" I ask, leaning back a little and nervously biting my lip.

"I've seen every one of your movies. I have dreams about you," he says as his fingers move across my shoulder.

"What kind of dreams?"

"We are on the beach that night. I relive it. It was one of the best nights of my life," he says sincerely.

"Hmm, I've dreamed about that night, too," I tell him. "But it had a much better ending."

"Can I kiss you again?" he asks.

"You'd freaking better. You don't know what I went through to get here."

He shuts me up by pressing his lips hard against mine. I let out a little moan and part my lips as he shoves his tongue into my mouth. I run my hand wildly through his hair and then find myself grabbing the hem of his shirt and pulling it off. It's then, while our lips are apart and he's stripping my shirt off, I see the same hunger I saw in his eyes that night on the beach. The same emotion. *How much different would our lives have been had we succumbed to that hunger then?*

But he wouldn't succumb even though I totally threw myself at him.

Repeatedly.

After what I've just been through, I can really appreciate a faithful man.

"You're even more beautiful than I remember," I tell him, my hands gliding from his broad shoulders, down his hard pecs, thick abs, and to a really impressive V-line. Troy might have been a hot rock star who left girls swooning in his wake, but I can tell you, he does not look anything like this.

Danny effortlessly picks me up and carries me to the bed. I grab his waistband and quickly unbutton his jeans, dying to see what's below. I used to stare at his underwear ads and think it would have been better marketing had he been naked, and the undies were lying on the floor.

Or maybe not. Heck, no one would have noticed the brand.

As I start to reach inside the boxer briefs that have girls chanting his name on more than game days, he stops me.

He shoves his hands through his hair. "It's all backward."

"You want me backward?" I start to turn around. I'm fine with doing anything he wants.

"No, I mean, *we're* all backward." He sits on the bed next to me, looking distressed. "I want you, Jennifer. God, I want you. Like, you have no idea how much I do. But I don't just want sex from you."

"What do you want?"

"I want you. In my life. For the rest of my life. You're supposed to ease into a relationship. You date, you get to know each other, you sleep together, and you get more serious. But things are different from when I was young. I have two kids. We have lives, careers, friends. We live in two different cities. The guy you were with for years cheated a little over a week ago. I was a wreck after Lori left me. I don't know what I would have done without Phillip and Jadyn."

"I don't know what I would have done without them either," I admit. "I don't have that many friends left, Danny."

"Do you get what I'm saying?" he asks. "Do you understand?"

"Yes, and no. The logical side of me understands what you're saying, but my heart feels like it did when you told me we couldn't talk anymore. It aches."

His hand moves to my chest, to the spot directly above my heart. "The last thing I want to do is cause you pain."

When his lips land on mine again, it feels like all his emotions and desire are funneled into the kiss.

"Wow," I say, taking a breath. "That might have been our best kiss so far."

"I don't want you to leave," he says, standing up and apparently needing to talk. "Are you just looking for a fling? Troy broke your heart, so you need to sleep with someone else to feel better? Because, if that's all you're looking for, I'm not that guy."

"Why not?" I ask. "You know we're going to have fun."

"Because I never wanted just a fling with you. I wanted your heart and soul and love."

"Do you still want that?" I ask, holding my breath in anticipation of his answer. Although my body is telling me all that matters is that we hook up, my heart has other ideas.

He sighs and runs his hand through his hair, like he doesn't know what to say.

"It's a simple question, Danny. Yes or no?" I stand up, ready to kick him out of here the second he says no. Because my heart can't take it.

His blue eyes settle on mine. He's breathing heavily and all worked up.

And I get it.

He's not divorced. I'm fresh out of a relationship. We do probably need time to heal. Things *are* all backward. We shouldn't have to think this hard about whether or not to take this next step. It's what we've both wanted. Based on the look on his face, I know that I am not going to like his answer.

But then his expression changes—his jaw set and his eyes squinted in bold determination.

"The answer is yes," he says, his muscular body launching toward me, fluidly picking me up as his lips slam against mine, and my back is pushed against the door.

The rest of the night is a flurry of emotions combined with the most incredible, fulfilling sex I've ever experienced. It's like all the love we feel, all the love we missed out on in the past, is wrapped into one highly combustible package and lit tonight, incinerating every other experience before it.

NOVEMBER 1ST

Danny

I WAKE UP in the most wonderful way—with Jennifer in my arms. Last night … *I can't even.* I remember telling Jadyn after I met Jennifer all those years ago that, if I'd slept with her, I would have never left the bed. That it would have been the most amazing sexual experience of my life. Fun combined with friendship mixed with passion and sex.

I kiss the top of her head and hug her tight, not wanting to let go. Not wanting to let this end. But I have to go. I have to get the kids up for school. I have to go to the attorney's office and face Lori.

Being a grownup sucks sometimes.

"That was something," she murmurs, her lips moving against my chest and her hand sliding down lower, causing me to harden again for about the thousandth time in the last twelve hours.

"You know, when I'm playing a game, I get to rest when the defense is on the field. I get time-outs. Halftime. I'm not sure I can do it again," I tease, because I so can.

The corners of her ruby lips curl into a smile as she naughtily dives her head under the covers. "Not in my game you don't."

AN HOUR LATER, we're collapsed in a heap and both breathing hard.

"So, do I get a ring for this?" she asks.

"Like an engagement ring?" I sputter out. Not that I don't want to marry her, but … "Um, I'm not divorced yet. I wouldn't want the kids—"

"I'm talking about the Championship of Sex Ring," she says with a smirk. "I was wondering if I'd won it yet."

I can't help but smile. I am so crazy about this girl. "Don't move. I'll be right back."

I hightail it out of bed, track down my clothes from where they are strewed across the floor, and get dressed.

When I get to my house, I'm happy to discover that my children are still asleep. I feel a pang of guilt about not being home last night. I know that I was next door. That I could literally see the house from where I was, but it feels incredibly irresponsible.

But so incredibly worth it.

I grab something from my closet and sneak back over to her room.

She's still lying in bed. The comforter is hanging off the side. The blanket that usually lies neatly across the foot of the bed is tossed over the chaise. And Jennifer looks beautiful, lying there. She has total sex hair. The soft pale skin of her shoulder is peeking out from under the covers. Part of me wonders if I am dreaming.

"Where did you go, Danny Diamond?" she purrs.

"I want to give you something." I perch on the edge of the bed.

When she sits up, the covers slide down her chest, revealing her beautiful breasts, which have a few love marks as a reminder of our night.

She grabs my shirt and pulls me close. "I'd say you gave me plenty last night, but I'm up for more."

I pull a box from behind my back and open the lid, revealing my first Championship ring. I take it out and slide it onto her thumb. "You definitely won the title."

Tears slide down her cheeks as she wraps her arms around my neck. "You are adorable, but I can't take this."

"I'm serious. I want you to have it. I'm going to win another one anyway."

"You are so cocky."

"If I recall, last night, you loved my *cock*iness."

"Yes, I did."

We kiss. Another perfect kiss.

"I need to get home and get the kids up and ready for school, but I was wondering if you'd like to go out tonight to celebrate the official announcement of my divorce."

"Uh-oh," she says, suddenly looking nervous. "I forgot to tell you. I'm going back home this morning."

"What?" I ask, my heart nearly stopping. "When were you going to tell me? After you left? So, that's all this was? You finally getting what you wanted? Me. For one night. Well, glad I could oblige."

"Wait, Danny. At the game Monday night, Tripp asked if I would come to LA with Jadyn," she says, talking fast, trying to explain, "and talk to his board about the hotel. So, that's today. And I felt like I had to say yes. I owe her that, I think. I mean, I have other things I have to do when I'm there, but—"

"Like what?" I ask flatly, even though I already know what she's going to say.

"Uh, I need to meet my agent and my assistant, find a place to live, and, well, I need to deal with Troy—"

"I see." I quickly force myself to my feet and burst out of her room. What more is there to say?

She's going home and not coming back. We're over again, before we ever got started.

IT'S NOT UNTIL later that I realize she left with my ring.

Will Jennifer and Danny find true love after getting sacked, or are they destined to watch from the sideline forever?

Read the next book in the That Boy series, *That Ring.*

ABOUT THE AUTHOR

Jillian Dodd is a *USA TODAY* bestselling author. She writes fun romances with characters her readers fall in love with—from the boy next door in the *That Boy* trilogy to the daughter of a famous actress in *The Keatyn Chronicles* series.

She is married to her college sweetheart, has two adult children, and has two Labs named Cali and Camber, and she lives in a small Florida beach town. When she's not working, she likes to decorate, paint, doodle, shop for shoes, watch football, and go to the beach.

www.jilliandodd.net